The subway train slowed down as it reached the station, but it was on the express track, so it couldn't stop.

A tall man, wearing a long cape, stood on a little platform on the end of the train. He stared at me and time seemed to stop. The train seemed frozen in place. I seemed to be frozen too, as if I were hypnotized or something.

I felt paralyzed and terrified all at the same time, and I didn't know why. The only thing I knew was that this guy was bad. *Evil.* But I couldn't look away. I was locked in his gaze.

He raised one long finger and pointed at me. Somewhere deep in my brain I screamed *No!*, but I took a step toward the tracks.

The man smiled, and his teeth dripped something dark onto the handrail. *Come closer. Closer.* I heard the words in my head as though he'd spoken them out loud. But his mouth didn't move. I took another step.

Suddenly, a light hit my eyes, dazzling me. Confusion roared in my head, but the voice kept calling. I stepped toward the edge of the platform. Right into the path of an oncoming train!

D1603000

SHADOW ZONE™

THE
UNDEAD
EXPRESS

BY J. R. BLACK

BULLSEYE BOOKS

Random House 🏠 New York

A BULLSEYE BOOK PUBLISHED BY RANDOM HOUSE, INC.

Copyright © 1994 by Twelfth House Productions. All rights reserved
under International and Pan-American Copyright Conventions.
Published in the United States by Random House, Inc., and
simultaneously in Canada by Random House of Canada Limited,
Toronto.
Library of Congress Catalog Card Number: 93-84907
ISBN: 0-679-85408-8
RL: 4.7

Manufactured in the United States of America   10 9 8 7 6 5 4 3 2 1

SHADOW ZONE is a trademark of Twelfth House Productions.

1

Ghost Train

It was Mick Masterson, class bully, who noticed the clock.

But it was me, Zach Kincaid, class chump, who took the dare.

It was the last class on Friday afternoon. We were all reading our *Short Stories to Read and Remember* book. Translation: the grinds like Allison Tulchin were reading while the rest of us daydreamed and doodled.

Even our English teacher, Mrs. Nowicki, was having a problem concentrating. She was supposedly marking papers, but her head kept dropping down and jerking up as she caught herself falling asleep. "Hey, Kincaid," Mick whispered. "Look at the clock."

I did. Kids always did what Mick Masterson told them to do. His nickname was the Mixmaster. Mick was about two feet taller than the tallest kid in sixth grade, not to mention a hun-

1

dred pounds heavier. Okay, maybe I'm exaggerating a little bit. But you get the picture, don't you?

"What about it?" I whispered back.

"It stopped," the Mixmaster said.

It was true. The clock read two-twenty, and when I looked at my watch, it was a quarter to three.

If anyone but the Mixmaster had said that, I would have said, Whoa, I'm impressed. You can actually tell time. But you didn't kid the Mixmaster. Not unless you wanted to get your face rearranged.

I just shrugged instead. "So?"

"So, you've got a watch on, right?" The Mixmaster had that gleam in his eye. The gleam that told you why he had his own personal chair in the principal's office. "Tell Nowicki that it's three o'clock. She's not wearing a watch. Maybe she'll let us off early."

"You're crazy," I said. "She'll *know*. Allison Tulchin will tell her."

"I'm sensing a major wimp factor here," Mick said. "*Major.*"

My dad is always telling me how a man of true courage doesn't do things because someone dares him. "Courage has to do with convictions," Dad says. "Not a herd mentality. You should watch cows sometime, Zach." This would be hard, considering we live right in the middle of New York City. But when Dad gets on a roll, I know better than to interrupt.

"Watch how when one cow breaks through a fence, they all follow. Then they all eat the wrong kind of grass and get sick." Dad grew up on a farm, so this story actually makes sense to him.

Not me. What can I say? I get up every day and go to middle school, not a pasture.

I cleared my throat. "Um, Mrs. Nowicki? The clock stopped."

Mrs. Nowicki gave a guilty start. She had finally settled into a good doze. "What was that, Zachary?"

"The clock. It stopped at two-twenty. It's one minute to three." I added the one minute. When you're stretching the truth, it's always a good idea to add details. People believe you then. I don't know why that is, but it is.

Allison Tulchin started to raise her hand, but Janie Russo grabbed a hank of her hair and pulled her back.

Mrs. Nowicki didn't even notice. She pushed up her glasses and tried to wake up. She blinked at me. "Oh. Thank you, Zachary. You can go, class. See you on Monday."

Everybody sprang out of their seats like they were hot-wired. The Mixmaster was the first to race out the door. He didn't even say thank you.

My best friend Gabrielle Lattanzi poked me in the back with a pencil. I twisted around and looked at her. Gabe had these big, round, light blue eyes that always showed what she was feeling. Right now it was a mixture of exasperation and worry.

"Why did you let the Mixmaster dare you like that?" she said as she stacked her books. "You'll be in trouble on Monday."

"Who cares," I said.

Gabe rolled her eyes. "*You* do, Kincaid."

"Do not."

"Do too," she said, grinning. Gabe and I had been friends since we were two, and sometimes we acted immature, just for fun.

We'd had no choice in becoming best friends, because our moms already were. My family had moved into the loft across the hall from the Lattanzis when I was a baby. Gabe and I used to spit up apple juice together while our moms did aerobics in front of the TV.

"Hurry up, you guys," came a whisper. It was J.T. Heffernan, our other best friend. "If Mrs. Nowicki figures out that Zach shaved fifteen

4

minutes off the time, he'll have to stay after school."

J.T.'s sandy brush cut seemed to vibrate. He was the nervous type, but he had a point. Stay after school on a Friday? No way!

We didn't relax until we were two blocks away from school. "So what's the plan, Stan?" J.T. asked. "What's up for Saturday? I say we check out comic books at Forbidden Planet."

"Sounds cool," Gabe agreed. "Then let's go for tacos at Lupe's. I haven't had Mexican food in three whole days."

"Count me out, you guys," I said. "It's an up weekend."

Gabe frowned. "I thought it was a down weekend."

I shook my head. "An up. No question."

An "up" weekend means I head uptown to spend Saturday and Sunday with my mom. A "down" weekend means I stay home with Dad in our loft on Franklin Street.

My parents got divorced last year. It hadn't exactly come as a shock. The trouble started when Mom became successful at her job. She worked in public relations, and all of a sudden, she started to get big clients and major bucks. My dad is a painter. He hangs around in old pants and teaches three days a week. My mom started wearing high heels and expensive suits and eating in fancy restaurants. My dad is a pizza and tacos kind of guy.

Not that my mom is a snob or anything. She's still funny and nice. But she just got tired of being poor, she said. The only trouble was, my dad *likes* being poor. Only he calls it "downscaling." Mom wanted me to live with her, too. But we all talked about it and decided I should stay downtown with my old friends and my old school.

So I look at it this way. I get the best of both worlds. On up weekends, I get to stay in a fancy apartment with a view of the East River. On down weekends, I get to hang around in my old clothes and eat pizza with my dad.

"Bummer," J.T. said. "An up weekend."

Even though Mom lives in a fabuloso apartment, I don't get to see her much. Lately, something always comes up. There's been a bunch of problems at work that's kept Mom bonding with telephones and fax machines. A couple of weeks earlier, I'd made the mistake of telling Gabe and J.T. the truth about my weekends uptown.

Now, Gabe and J.T., they put on these real sad faces, like they were sorry for me, everytime they heard I was going uptown. I can't stand people feeling sorry for me. Besides, it made me feel like I'd somehow been disloyal to my mom.

"No way," I told Gabe and J.T. "It's going to be a totally stellar weekend. Mom got us tickets to the Knicks game. She pulled some strings and we're going to sit in this special section right up front. They bring drinks and hot dogs right to your seat and everything's *free*."

"Whoa," J.T. said. "Maximum cool."

"They're playing the Bulls, too," Gabe said.

"Well, I've got to hit the road," I said. I didn't really meet their eyes.

Gabe and J.T. were my best friends and we'd made it through some major bummer periods together. Like when Gabe's little brother, Piero, was born and, suddenly, Gabe had to babysit all the time. Or when J.T. had an appendicitis attack the day we'd rented all three Star Wars movies. And when J.T. decided to change his name from Jeremiah Taos, Gabe and I had trained ourselves to call him by his initials. Then there was the time Gabe was chosen to play Persephone, goddess of spring, in the class pageant. J.T. and I didn't even make fun of her, even when she had to wear a crown of plastic flowers. Now *that's* loyalty.

Still, I didn't want them to know that my mom never had time for me anymore. So even though I hadn't meant to lie to them about going

7

to the Knicks game, it had just come out that way.

I said goodbye and walked over to Hudson Street to the video store. My mom usually has a stack of boring videos waiting for me. So it's up to me to pick up something watchable, something Mom or Dad would never let me rent in a million years. I have my very own VCR in my bedroom uptown, and Mom wouldn't be around anyway.

Maximum cool! *Blood Curse of the Vampire* was in. I gave my card to the guy and tucked it in my backpack. It was still pretty light. I didn't have to pack when I went to Mom's. I had clothes and pajamas and another toothbrush up there.

I walked up to Canal Street to catch the Number 6 train. It wasn't rush hour yet, and I was the only one on the platform. I'd never admit it to Gabe or J.T., but I get a little spooked if I'm the only one in a subway station. There's something about the dark corners and the tracks glinting in the gloom that gives me the willies.

I whistled under my breath until I heard the sound of the train. Finally!

But then the weirdest looking train chugged out of the tunnel. It had only one car, with a strange squarish roof and small doors. It looked old-fashioned, like it belonged in the transit museum.

The train slowed down as it reached the station, but it was on the express track, so it couldn't stop.

I watched the train go by as if it were moving in slow motion. The light must have been weird inside the car, because the faces behind the windows all looked chalk-white. They all moved in slow motion, too, as they turned their heads to stare at me. Their expressions were blank and their eyes looked dead.

A tall man, wearing a long cape, stood on a little platform on the end of the train. His face was pale and shining. He tossed something in my direction. I watched it fly slowly toward me. It landed at my feet. It was a rat. A dead one. Blood trickled out in a tiny stream from its body.

Everything still felt slow to me, even as I gasped and jumped back. I looked up at the guy. He stared back at me and time seemed to stop. The train seemed frozen in place. I seemed to be frozen too, as if I were hypnotized or something.

A sickly sweet odor hit me like a wave. I felt paralyzed and terrified all at the same time, and I didn't know why. The only thing I knew was that this guy was bad. *Evil.* But I couldn't look

9

away. I was locked in his gaze.

He raised one long, bony finger and pointed at me. Somewhere deep in my brain I screamed *No!*, but I took a step toward the tracks. Then I took another.

The man smiled, and his teeth dripped something dark and wet onto the handrail. *Come closer. Closer.* I heard the words in my head as though he'd spoken them out loud. But his mouth didn't move. The voice sounded soothing. Warm. But something about it made me sick, like the smell. I took another step.

Suddenly, a light hit my eyes, dazzling me. Confusion roared in my head, but the voice kept calling. I stepped toward the edge of the platform. Right into the path of an oncoming train!

2

Blood Curse

"Watch out, buddy!"

My collar was yanked tight, and I was jerked backward. I turned and saw a guy in a parka shaking his head at me. "You almost killed yourself, kid," he shouted at me over the roar of the train. "You'd better pay attention."

"Did you see it?" I asked shakily. I was trembling all over.

"What?" the man said back to me.

"That—that *thing,*" I said.

"It's just a rat," the man said, stepping over it. "Relax. And keep your eyes open, kid."

He shouldered past me as the train doors whooshed open. I jumped on after him.

I sat down and stared at the floor, trying to catch my breath. That guy on the weird train had looked like a vampire. A vampire on a train full of dead people. I clenched my hands together so they would stop shaking. I *couldn't* have seen what I saw. But I had!

I watched the stations go by and people get on and off. Suddenly, the world seemed like a scary place where anything could happen. I was completely spooked.

It took me all the way to 33rd Street to figure out what had happened. I must have stumbled on a movie shoot! People were always filming movies or commercials in Manhattan. I'd probably seen a bunch of actors dressed up as ghosts. Maybe they were making some sort of funny commercial. I hadn't seen any cameras, but they could have been on the train. And I had just imagined everything else—the spooky voice in my head, the funny smell. Mom always said I had an overactive imagination.

I was so relieved that I burst out laughing. This was probably not a great idea, since I was on a crowded subway car. Everybody looked at me, then quickly looked away. The lady sitting next to me moved over as much as she could. She looked like my father's Aunt Marge, who always sniffed when she saw his paintings and said she guessed she wasn't smart enough to understand them.

The lady moved over so far she nearly sat on some guy's lap. Then *he* inched over and knocked his head against some man's briefcase.

That made me chuckle, which only made things worse.

As long as I had embarrassed myself, I might as well have some fun. I kept on chuckling like a maniac. I stood up and laughed like the madman in *House of Blood.* Then the train pulled into my stop, and I jumped off, still cackling.

"Kids today," I heard a man say as the doors closed.

I have to say, Mom really made an effort that weekend. She even cooked dinner Friday night. It wasn't her fault that she had to get on a conference call to "the coast"—that's what she called Los Angeles—and left the spaghetti on the stove too long. She dumped a clump of it on my plate. It just sat there, like a hat.

"How is it?" she asked, anxiously watching me take a bite.

I chewed and swallowed. It was the worst spaghetti I'd ever tasted. "It's great," I said. Mom leaned back, relieved, and took a sip of wine. "What do you call this, anyway?" I asked. "Pasta a la Elmer's?"

Mom looked blank for a minute. Then she got the joke. Here's the thing about her—when she laughs, she really laughs. She choked on her wine and leaned back in the chair, letting out funny whoops that ended in a giggle.

"You're a monster," she said to me. "Hand me those takeout menus. We'll order some pizza."

You see? She's not so bad. We had such a good time Friday night that I didn't really mind on Saturday when she canceled Rollerblading in the park and went to her office. And I *almost* didn't mind when she called home and said she couldn't have dinner with me.

But I *did* mind when she called her old friend Mimi Milgrim to see if her son, Jeffrey, would like to watch TV with me. Jeffrey came up and wanted to watch three dumb shows in a row. He ate most of the M&Ms and picked his nose right in front of me. I didn't even *touch* the M&Ms after that. Jeffrey Milgrim was the mondo-est Mondo Dweeb I'd ever had the displeasure to meet.

The only fun I had Saturday was after Jeffrey left and Mom came home and went to bed. That's when I slipped *Blood Curse of the Vampire* into the VCR and watched the whole thing. I didn't close my eyes once, even when the girl and the guy open the vampire's coffin to kill him with a huge stake through his heart. Maximum cool!

On Sundays, Mom and I have one unbreakable date: bagels at Barney Greengrass, The Sturgeon King, on Amsterdam Avenue. Then we walk home through the park. Luckily, this Sunday Mom didn't drag me to some art exhibit. Instead, she read the paper while I flipped on the football game. And then it was time to go home.

Mom kissed me goodbye at the door and then hugged me extra hard since I wouldn't see her for two weeks.

"Did you have an okay time?" she asked. She looked a little anxious, so of course I told her it was maximum cool.

"Sorry about the spaghetti," she said.

"Don't sweat it, Mom. The pizza was great," I said.

"Next time, I'll cook a big meal," she said. "Chicken, potatoes, salad, and that fried zucchini that you like. Then we'll go out to a movie or something."

"Sounds great," I said. I knew it wouldn't happen, but sometimes you have to play along with parents. Especially busy, successful ones.

"Here," she said, handing me a ten. "Have Max call you a cab, okay?" Max is the doorman. He's about a hundred years old.

"Sure, Mom," I said. Every time I went there, it was the same routine. She gave me the ten. I told her I'd take a cab. And then I pocketed it and made for the subway.

I said goodbye and headed down in the elevator. "See you in a couple of weeks!" I called to Max.

"No, I think it looks like rain," he said.

I started walking toward Lexington Avenue But when I got to the stop for the Number 6 train, I saw Jeffrey Milgrim heading down the stairs. I stopped in my tracks. No way was I going to share the platform with Mondo Dweeb! Then I'd actually have to ride with him too. Talk about minimum cool!

So I kept on walking south. It was a nice afternoon, not too chilly, and I only had my backpack to carry. I knew I could pick up the train at Grand Central.

If you've never been to New York, you probably don't know this, but Grand Central Terminal is gigantic. It was built almost a hundred years ago, and the main concourse has a ceiling that's got to be a hundred feet high. I'm not exaggerating here. Every time I walk through it, my thoughts seem to fly up and away. I like to tilt my head back and circle around, staring at the ceiling high above and looking for pigeons. That usually makes me dizzy.

What I'm trying to say is, I got lost and it wasn't *completely* my fault. I wasn't paying attention, and like I said, my thoughts were still floating above the main concourse. I thought I was following signs to the Number 6 train, but I ended up in a part of the station I'd never seen before. And there was nobody around to ask directions.

I was sure that I'd find another sign ahead, so I kept on walking. Finally, down a long, deserted corridor and around a bend, I saw a mosaic sign that said: SUBWAY. It looked like the mosaic was being repaired, since there was a construction barrier that I had to squeeze around.

I headed down a long, dark tunnel. It was definitely creepy, but subway tunnels usually are. I couldn't help thinking about *Blood Curse of the Vampire,* when the hero is trapped in a cemetery vault in the basement of the vampire's castle. It made me wish that I'd used Mom's ten and taken a cab back downtown.

I went under a grating that flooded a square of light onto the floor. Then the tunnel turned left sharply. Ahead of me, through the gloom, I saw someone coming toward me. It was a man dressed in a dark blue shirt and matching pants. He was wearing a cap, and I realized that he was a subway maintenance worker. Great! He'd know if I was on the right track. Ha ha.

I couldn't really see the guy, since he was in deep shadow. "Hey," I called. "Do you know if the subway stop is back that way?"

The man didn't answer. He stopped.

"I'm looking for the Number 6 train," I said.

"I'll show you," the man said. He moved past me, and I shrank back against the tunnel wall. I smelled the same smell as the other day, like fruit going rotten.

"Come," he said.

Come. That word again, spoken in the same hypnotic way. It gave me a creepy feeling, but I shook it off. I followed the guy down the tunnel, back the way I'd come.

We turned that sharp corner, into that dazzling light that shone through the grating overhead. Suddenly, the man staggered. He tried to move out of the light, but it was like he was rooted to the spot. His hands flew into the air and the light seemed to stream through his skin. His hands looked like they belonged to a skeleton—all bones.

Slowly, he turned around. The skin on his face was melting, and I saw a death's-head staring at me. A skull with burning coals for eyes. Blood dripped from his long teeth. Now *I* couldn't move. The skeleton hands reached for me, and I started to scream.

3

Introducing: The Undead

Hands shot out from behind me and grabbed the subway worker's shoulders. He was yanked past me, back into the darkness. I heard a thud, and when I turned, he was slumped on the floor. His head was in his hands. There was skin on his hands again, but I could *almost* see the bones.

"Wh—wh—wh—" The sounds came out of me in little gasps. I couldn't talk. If my legs could have moved, I would have run away.

The man who had grabbed the subway worker was tall and elegant. His face shone dimly through the darkness, pale as a February moon. I noticed that he was wearing a cape and carrying a cane. The guy looked like a magician. All he needed was a rabbit.

"Don't be afraid," he said smoothly. He clicked his heels together. "Valentine Cutter, at your service, sir."

"What happened?" I managed to gasp. "Why

did that guy . . . I mean, did I see what I *think* I saw?"

"And what do you think you saw, young man?"

"A skull," I said. I shuddered. "I know it sounds crazy, but . . ." Then I remembered where I'd seen Valentine Cutter before. "Wait a second," I said. "You're that guy. The guy on the train who threw the rat at me." I squinted at him. My heartbeat was returning to normal as I figured the whole thing out. "So are you guys shooting a movie, or what?"

"A movie," Valentine Cutter repeated slowly.

"Or are you guys magicians? Look, I don't care. I'm just trying to find the Number 6 train," I said. "Now I wish I'd walked home."

Suddenly, the man on the floor spoke up. "Don't let him go," he rasped. "I promised Sims. He paid me three rats—"

"Be quiet, Dwayne!" Valentine Cutter said sharply. He gave me a smile that was more like a wince. "Dwayne wants to apologize for scaring you. Don't you, Dwayne?"

There was a long pause. Then the man looked up at me. His face looked normal again. Pale, and a little on the caveman side, but normal. That must have been some makeup job. "Sure. Sorry."

"Excellent," Valentine Cutter said. "Now, young man, you are looking for the train. May I suggest that you follow me, sir?"

Sir? Was this guy in the military?

Dwayne staggered to his feet, and he followed behind us, limping a little. Behind me, I heard *step, drag, step, drag,* just like in a horror movie. Maybe Dwayne was still trying to scare me.

I couldn't wait to tell Gabe and J.T. about this experience. I'd leave *out* the part about them being actors or magicians, though. You shoulda seen this pair. I'm talking homicidal maniacs! I'd say. I'd exaggerate just a little bit. I could just see Gabe's blue eyes get rounder and rounder as I told her about Valentine Cutter's dead-white face and the skull that had been Dwayne's face. The skull that drooled blood, I would say.

The three of us walked down the tunnel. I guess I should have asked about the movie, but I couldn't. To be honest, I was still shaken up.

As we turned a corner, I saw a train sitting at the platform, its doors open.

"You'd better hurry," Valentine Cutter said.

I hesitated. "Are you catching this one?"

"No," Valentine Cutter said. "My friend and I will wait. *Bon voyage.*"

"Right," I said, jogging toward the train. I

hopped on it with relief. I wanted to be around people again. Normal people, that is.

There was a seat across the aisle, and I sat down just as the train lurched forward. The car was about halfway full. Something was funny about the passengers, though. I couldn't see very well because the lights in the train were really dim. I looked up. There was just a tiny bulb in a little cage above my head, and it was flickering. I'd never seen lights like that on a subway train before. And the seat was upholstered. It wasn't plastic.

I looked at the other passengers more carefully. The woman across from me was wearing little boots that buttoned up the side. Those were in style these days. And she was wearing an ankle-length skirt. That could have been in style, too, I guess, especially in *my* neighborhood. But then I looked up at her face. She was wearing this tiny velvet hat with ribbons that tied under the chin. She looked like she could have been in a photograph of Old New York.

Next to her was a guy in a suit and hat who could have stepped out of a movie from the forties. And next to *him* was this long-haired hippie who was wearing sandals and a fringed suede vest. On the other side of the woman was a man wearing a flat-topped straw hat with a striped ribbon and a weird suit. His shirt had a stiff, round collar. I peeked at the newspaper he was reading. The *New York Herald.* I hadn't heard of the *New York Herald* before. I squinted to read the date. It said October 30, *1929!*

I let out a long breath. It must be a prop. They must be actors from the same movie shoot. But why were they all dressed in clothes from different eras? Why hadn't Dwayne and Valentine Cutter climbed aboard?

The tunnel seemed to go on forever. Why hadn't we come to a stop yet?

I turned to the man next to me to ask him if the train was going downtown. When I saw his face, I gulped in shock. It was Valentine Cutter! It couldn't be. I'd left him behind. I'd run right past him, and nobody had gotten on the train after me.

He couldn't be here. But here he was.

"So we meet again," he said.

"Uh, hi," I said. "Is this train heading downtown, do you know?"

"I believe so."

"Good," I said, relieved. "Do you know if it stops at Canal Street?"

"Not anymore," Mr. Cutter said. He smiled. Two of his teeth were awfully long and pointed. This guy definitely needed a good dentist.

"What did he say?" the guy with the straw hat asked above the rattle of the train. He had a thin, mean face with eyes like pebbles.

"He wanted to know if the train stops at Canal Street," Valentine Cutter said.

All the passengers began to laugh, like this was the funniest thing they had ever heard.

"Wait a second," I said. "Don't tell me this train goes to *Queens.*"

This made them laugh even harder. Their eyes shone, and their pointed teeth glistened. Their pale faces seem to glow with a greenish light in the gloom. Then I noticed Dwayne was there, almost hidden behind a guy in a uniform that looked like it came from World War I. Dwayne had the most obnoxious laugh of all.

"So what's going on?" I asked Mr. Cutter. I have to admit, my voice cracked a little. I was just a little bit nervous. "Are you guys on your way to a movie shoot? Or a TV show?"

"TV?" Mr. Cutter asked.

"Television," the hippie said. "I told you about it, man. Junk, mostly. But 'Gilligan's Island' is a trip."

"Ah. The little box full of plays. Yes, I remember." Mr. Cutter nodded several times.

"Box full of plays," I said. "Very funny. You know, when I saw this train the other day, I thought it was a ghost train. You guys really spooked me. Ha ha. I thought it was a train full of dead people. Funny, huh?"

Valentine chuckled. "Close, but no cigar," he said. He leaned closer to me. "Not *dead* people. Not dead at all."

"Glad to hear it," I said, grinning.

"*Un*dead," Valentine said.

I couldn't have heard right. I leaned a little closer. "What did you say?"

"The *undead*," Valentine said. He spread his arms to include everyone in the subway car. His eyes seemed to burn with a steady fire. "We are not alive. We are not dead. But we feed on the blood of the living."

Okay, I'm a city kid. I've got street smarts. But even though I *knew* this crazy guy was just trying to shake me up, I couldn't ignore it. I was scared.

"What's the matter, Zachary? Don't you know about the *nosferatu?*"

"The nose-for-what?" I asked, trying to joke away my fear. Then my blood ran cold. "Hey, wait a second. How did you know my name?"

"*Nosferatu,* Zachary," Valentine repeated. "The undead. We are all vampires. And we'd like to welcome you to the Undead Express!"

4

Ride to Nowhere

The expression on my face must have been hysterical, because Valentine started to laugh. He leaned back and I saw his long, pointed teeth glinting. That's when I jumped up with a cry that sounded like I was strangling. My pants caught on some kind of nail and I ripped them away. I had to get away from this guy!

I moved to the other side of the car. Didn't this train ever *stop?* I hung onto the pole and looked out into the darkness rushing by. No way was I going to even *glance* at Valentine Cutter again.

I felt something brush against my leg. The woman in the funny hat was reaching toward the torn part of my pants. I looked down and saw that I had a long scratch. Blood was trickling down my calf. Before I could move, the woman reached out and touched the blood with her finger. Then she brought the finger back to her mouth and licked it! Her eyes closed, as though she had just tasted a hot fudge sundae.

I jumped back and hit my head on the door. A shudder went through my whole body. Talk about gross!

Suddenly, Valentine stood up and unfurled his cape. The red satin lining seemed to give his face a bloody tinge. "He's mine!" Valentine rasped. He flapped his cape at the woman and she shrank back, hissing.

My legs were shaking so badly I didn't know if I could keep standing. I looked around the car. All of the passengers had their greedy eyes fastened on me. The mean-looking man in the straw hat licked his lips.

"Do not worry, my friend," Valentine said smoothly as he came up to me. He took my arm and steered me down to an empty seat at the end of the car. "You are under my protection."

"I am? Why?" I noticed that my hands were shaking, so I sat on them. Then my legs started to shake. "I mean, why should they listen to you? Who *are* you? Who are *they?*"

"They listen to me because I am the First," Valentine said. "Without me they would not know the pleasures of the Shadow Zone."

"The what?" I asked.

"The Shadow Zone," Valentine said. He gestured toward the car. "As vampires, we inhabit this place. It is somewhere between what is real and what is not. Somewhere between what is known and what is only imagined. And you are lucky to have stumbled upon it, Zachary."

Lucky? He must be nuts! "See, that's what I'm talking about," I said. "How do you know my name?"

Valentine shrugged. "In the Shadow Zone, we know many things. Things we do not have to learn."

"Boy," I said, "that could come in handy in math class."

Valentine chuckled. He put a hand on my arm and I flinched. It was so *cold!* "I like you, Zachary," he said.

"Wish I could say the same," I muttered, and Valentine laughed again. How do you like that, a vampire with a sense of humor.

"You said you were the first," I said. "What does that mean?"

"Ah, yes." Valentine took his hand away. What a relief! It was starting to feel like my arm had been stuck in the freezer. He leaned on the top of his cane. "I entered the world of the undead in 1905."

"Wait a second," I said. "1905? That was

almost a hundred years ago."

Valentine nodded, as if that was perfectly normal. "I was a prosperous gentleman living on Fifth Avenue. I had a fifty-room house built of white limestone. I kept two carriages. I summered in Newport."

"Are you trying to tell me that you were loaded?" I asked.

"If you mean to ask if I was a millionaire, yes," Valentine said with a slight nod. "I made my money in railroads. When the idea for an underground railway was proposed, I was one of the first to support it. I was one of the men who raised bonds to pay for it, one of the men who built it, and ultimately, one of the men who profited from it. Because of that, I made it a point to ride it everywhere—even to the opera."

Valentine indicated his cane and his cloak. "I'll never forget that night," he said, his voice dropping to a rhythm that seemed to mimic the train wheels. I felt awake and asleep at the same time, like when Mr. Potasher, my social studies teacher, tries to explain how the system of checks and balances works in the U.S. government.

"It was undeniably the greatest night of my life," Valentine went on, his eyes glittering.

"Down here, in the caverns beneath the city, I met my fate. Barnabus welcomed me to the world of the undead."

"Barnabus was a . . . a vampire?"

"He was more than a thousand years old," Valentine said. "He knew all. He had walked the world for centuries."

"Which one is he?" I asked, twisting around.

Valentine bowed his head. "He is . . . no more. He was not content with our life underground. He took the route that Dwayne tried. But I was not so quick to save him. A few minutes of light and . . . well, you saw what almost happened to Dwayne."

"Yeah," I said. "Unfortunately."

"Dwayne was lucky," Valentine said. "He wasn't caught long enough for the effects to last. He knew his chances. Every so often, someone gets impatient, and tries to find his or her way out. They have all gotten caught in the light." He shrugged. "At least it helps with overcrowding."

"That's one way to look at it, I guess," I said.

"They are fools," Valentine said. "Why should they risk losing the mystery and power of the undead? Blood is our food and drink, and immortality is our prize!"

His eyes bored into mine. I felt myself

falling. But I wasn't moving. It just *felt* like I was falling, down into the blackness of Valentine's gaze.

I don't know what would have happened if a mouse hadn't run over my foot just then. It made a squeaking noise, and I must have jumped a mile.

For once, I was happy to see a rodent. I felt like I'd just woken up from a dream.

"Whoa," I said. "Just hold it. Do you really think I'm *buying* this? You're a magician, right? And you just tried to hypnotize me. Let me tell you, bud, it didn't work. I'm not believing this for one—"

Suddenly, I heard the *eeeeek* of the mouse again. Only this time it was more frantic. I looked across the aisle. The guy in the straw hat had scooped up the mouse in his hand. He raised it to his mouth and bit off the head, just like it was a Fig Newton or something.

I whipped my head back and looked at the floor until my stomach stopped churning. *They are vampires,* I thought with horror. *They really are.*

Then I felt a terror that paralyzed me. I could think. But I couldn't move.

"Don't be afraid, Zachary," Valentine said. "Didn't I tell you that you were under my protection? Let me ask you something. Why do you think that what you know is all there is? The world is a wide place, with room for many different things. Wonderful things. Didn't you ever wonder about the dark?"

"Sure, when I was six," I said. "I used to think a monster lived in my closet. But I grew up."

I looked out the window. Why didn't we pass any stations? Where were we going? How could I get off this train?

"The train runs on very old tracks," Valentine said, as if he'd read my mind. "They are so old that the transit authority doesn't use them. They don't even inspect them. Once, we were able to come and go at will. But now, the tracks cross over into an existing subway line at only one place—where you first saw us. We're on an express track, so we can't stop there. We ride in eternal night, below the heart of the city."

"But how do you—" I stopped and gulped. I wanted to say *How do you get fresh victims?* But I couldn't get the words out.

"How do we introduce others to our magical world?" Valentine asked. He shrugged. "People get lost. That tunnel in Grand Central has been very . . . fruitful. And of course, there are the rest of the train tunnels. Once in a great while a worker will get lost. And there are the rats.

Some of my friends don't care for them, but I find them delicious. It's humans I don't care for." Valentine shuddered. "Something about all that warmth, that life . . . it's too rich for me."

I gazed at him, fascinated. He might have been talking about pot roast.

"I guess you could call me a vegetarian," Valentine said, smiling.

I wished he wouldn't smile. When I didn't see those pointed teeth, I could almost forget that he was a bloodsucking vampire.

The other vampires on the train had gathered into a little knot. They were talking in low voices and looking over at me. Somehow, I wasn't crazy about the *way* they were looking.

"What's going on?" I asked Valentine. "They don't look too happy."

"They are hungry," Valentine said flatly. "They want humans."

"What do *you* want?" I asked.

Valentine sighed. "I have to tell you, Zachary. After a couple of decades or so, you start to get bored with your companions. It's the same conversations, over and over. Take Ronnie over there, in the headband and vest. The one who looks like Buffalo Bill."

Oh. The long-haired hippie.

Valentine rolled his eyes. "All I hear about is

peace, love, the Rolling Stones, over and over. I could scream. And Pearl, in the hat. She took a trip to Niagara Falls in 1903 and she's *still* talking about it. Oh, and there's Sims, in the boater. The straw hat," Valentine explained. "He won't shut up about the stock market crash in 1929. He should have sold short, blah blah blah. You can imagine the boredom. Vampires are people too, you know. I miss Barnabus. At least he was interesting. The people he'd known! I understand Attila the Hun was a charming man."

I frowned. "Somehow, I don't feel real sympathetic, Valentine. I mean, it's hard to feel sorry for a vampire."

He touched my shoulder, and I could feel the coldness of his fingers. "I need to know where the tunnels lead," he said. "And, more important, I need to know whether it's day or night. There are no clocks in the old stations. There's no way to tell time. Now and then we've sent out scouts to check and see if there's light coming through the grates. The few who returned were disfigured or blind."

Valentine leaned closer. Again, his eyes seemed to glow red, bringing me down into a dark, sweet place. "So, tell me, Zachary. Where does the tunnel lead? Is it night right now? Tell me."

I was mesmerized. But at the same time, a part of my brain was screaming *NO*. Part of me had figured out that if I told Valentine the truth, the vampires would be let loose on Grand Central. And from the station, they could get on almost any subway line. I would be responsible for letting loose a trainful of vampires on New York City!

"Tell me, Zachary. Tell me."

I was drowning. He was pulling me down. And it was so warm and pleasant where I was going, down to a place of rich ruby blood . . .

"NO!" I shouted. I stood up. "No!" I looked around wildly.

"Give him to us!" Pearl shrieked.

"He's ours, Valentine!" Sims snarled.

As they began to move toward me, they fanned out in a semicircle. In just another moment, they'd have me surrounded! And I knew with a sickening feeling that even Valentine wouldn't be able to save me.

5

The Boy Who Cried Vampire

The train lurched, and I threw out my hands to steady myself. My hand hit a cord.

The emergency cord.

I looked out the window and saw that we were approaching a station. There was no one standing on the platform. There wasn't even a token booth. But I didn't care. I pulled the cord, hard, and the train shuddered as it screeched to a stop.

I had braced myself so I didn't fall over, but the vampires went down like bowling pins.

"Get off me!" Pearl shrieked.

"Ow!" Ronnie cried. "You're on my hair!"

I dashed to the doors and dug my fingers in the crack. I saw the vampire conductor hurry toward the little compartment up front to start the train again. I tugged frantically, and the doors gave. I pulled them open and jumped out onto the platform just as the train began to move. The closing doors snapped at the tail of my jacket.

As the train rolled slowly by me, I looked in the window. Valentine was standing alone in the middle of the aisle. The rest of the ghouls were probably still tangled up on the floor.

This is the weirdest part: I could tell that Valentine was laughing. Not in a mean way, either. He was just chuckling, like my dad did at a really good joke. Then he winked at me as the train rolled away.

I stood there, shaking. I admit it: I was scared right down to my socks. *You* try sitting with a trainful of vampires. See what it does to *your* nerves.

The train disappeared into the tunnel. I was never so glad to see the back of anything in my life.

Finally I gulped and looked around. I was standing in a dark, empty station. There was trash lying around that looked like it had been there a long time. There was no sign saying which station this was. But the station was incredible, like none I'd ever seen. The ceilings were high and curved. The beams had designs of vines and leaves in the metalwork.

I walked over to the wall. I could just barely make out letters that spelled out two words in different colored tiles. I used the bottom of my T-shirt to wipe away the grime:

CITY HALL

It was the City Hall station. But I'd been in the City Hall station, and this wasn't it. Obviously, this one had been abandoned. I just hoped there was a way out.

It took me fifteen minutes of prowling around and being spooked by rustling noises—unlike Valentine, I'm not fond of rats—to find the exit. It was up a long flight of stairs, and then I had to push aside some boards and squeeze through a tiny space. I lost two buttons off my denim jacket.

But I was out. I breathed fresh air, and it felt great. The sun was slanting low in the sky, and I was late for dinner. I found Broadway and hurried north toward home.

When I got home, I smelled garlic. Dad was stir-frying something on the stove. We must be having his special Chinese dinner, spicy stir-fried vegetables over noodles. Actually, it was pretty good, especially with lots of soy sauce.

When Dad heard the bang of the door, he yelled hello and kept stirring. I could see him because the kitchen wasn't a separate room. A long counter divided it from the rest of the space.

A loft is just a huge open room, basically, with superhigh ceilings. Our building used to be a clothing factory. They even used to make Civil War uniforms in our loft. The only rooms that were separate were our bedrooms and the bathroom. Dad and Mom had built the walls themselves when we moved in.

"Hey, Zach. You're late. Did you have a nice—" Dad looked up and dropped the spatula as I came into the kitchen. "What happened? Are you okay?" he asked, coming toward me anxiously.

I looked down at myself. My jacket was filthy from squeezing through the boards, and my pants had that big rip in them. I got a look at my face in the toaster, and it didn't look any better. There was a huge streak of dirt across one cheek. Besides that, I looked awfully pale. Not as white as the vampires had been, but close.

"I'm fine," I said. "But boy, did I have a weirdsville ride on the subway." I knew I couldn't tell my dad *everything*. He's pretty cool, but he's still a dad. He'd probably forbid me to ever ride the subway again.

Dad turned off the flame under the pan.

Even in times of crisis, he didn't neglect dinner. No way would he let the vegetables get mushy. "What happened?" he asked.

"There was this creepy guy on the subway," I said. "He said he was a vampire. And he had these really long, pointed teeth. He said everybody *else* was a vampire, too. And the train wouldn't stop, Dad! It just kept on going and going, like that Energizer bunny."

Dad frowned. "You must have been on the express."

"Exactly! The Undead Express," I said.

Dad grinned. "Catchy, Zach. But come on. Vampires?" He frowned at me. "Did you rent one of those movies you're not allowed to rent, by any chance?"

I looked around guiltily for my backpack, and that's when it hit me: I left it on the train.

"My backpack," I said. "It's gone. I mean, I guess I left it on the train."

Now Dad looked annoyed. "Zach, that backpack cost fifty dollars. Remember, you *had* to have the one that you could take camping in subzero temperatures? Even though you haven't been camping since you were six years old?"

"I didn't mean to forget it," I said. "I was *scared*, Dad. I'm trying to tell you."

"Some jerk was trying to frighten you," Dad

said. "I've told you a million times to get on the car that has the conductor. If somebody bothers you, tell him."

I wanted to tell Dad that I *was* on the car with the conductor. Only *this* conductor liked to feast on human blood.

"That's the other weird thing," I said instead. "There was only one car."

Now Dad *really* looked irritated. "Don't start with me, Zachary. There isn't a subway in New York that only has one—" The phone rang next to his hand, and he sighed. "Don't go anywhere."

Dad picked up the phone. "Oh, hello, Ellie," he said. It was my mom. "Yes, he just got home. No, no, he ran into some jerk on the subway, and—what?" There was a long pause. Dad started drumming his fingers on the kitchen counter. "No, I didn't know that. Well, how could I? Now that you moved uptown you don't believe in public transportation anymore? No, that was not a crack. It was—what?"

I shrugged out of my jacket. This was going to take a while. My dad and mom tried to have extremely limited contact these days. They both knew that within five minutes, they'd start arguing. This time, it had only taken five *seconds*.

The trouble is, I think Mom still feels guilty that I'm not living with her. So she's a little overprotective. And my dad gets defensive if he thinks she's criticizing him.

What can I say? It's a mess.

I went to the bathroom and washed my hands and face. The cool water calmed me down a little bit. Then I changed my T-shirt and torn jeans. I could hear Dad still arguing in the kitchen. How about that. You escape from a trainful of vampires, and home doesn't even feel safe.

I made a wall of pillows on the bed, just like I had when I was a kid, pretending that the pillows made a fort. Only now I knew that danger was a lot closer than I'd ever dreamed. And a whole lot scarier.

But had it been *real?* They *couldn't* have been vampires. Valentine must have been a magician. That mouse the other guy bit was probably a fake mouse he used in his act. And Dwayne was probably wearing some weird makeup when he stepped into that light. Then he wiped it off when his head was in his hands. If they'd tried to scare me, they'd done a terrific job. But at least I'd have a good story to tell Gabe and J.T.

Dad poked his head in my room. "Hungry?"

I sat up and shrugged. "Sure. I guess so."

"It'll be ready in a minute." Dad stuck his hands in his jeans pockets. He always feels guilty after he argues with Mom. "Listen, Zach. If your mom gives you cab fare, will you do me a favor and *take* a cab from now on? She doesn't want you to take the subway for such a long ride."

"Okay," I said.

"I didn't tell her you'd been taking the subway every weekend," Dad said. "I didn't think it was . . . uh, wise. So why have you been pocketing the money?"

"I run out of my allowance around Thursday," I said. As soon as the words were out of my mouth, I wanted to kick myself. Dad's face fell. I knew he couldn't afford to give me any more money. And he'd have to talk to Mom about raising it. She could say yes right away because she could swing it, no problem. Dad knew that as well as I did. I was a jerk for reminding him that Mom probably made fifty times as much money as he did.

I knew it bothered him that Mom had such a swanky place and we lived in a dump. The thing is, I *liked* our loft. It was funky and comfortable, full of big couches and lots of room. When I was younger, I used to roller skate in the living room. I kid you not.

"I'll talk to your mom about raising it," he said.

43

"Don't bother, Dad," I said. "Really. I'll just cut back on sodas and stuff."

He nodded, but I could tell he wasn't really listening. "Did you have fun this weekend?" he asked. "Ellie said she's been busy with work. You got to spend time with her, didn't you?"

Uh-oh. Major trap. There was no way I'd let my Dad know how much time I spent alone when I was at Mom's. I wasn't going to give them something else to fight about. When they first split up, I used to wish really hard for them to get back together. Now I only wished they could carry on a conversation.

"Sure, I had fun," I said. "It was maximum cool."

The timer went off in the kitchen. "Chow time," Dad said. "And then how about a game of Scrabble? That will chase those vampires away."

"Yeah," I said.

But I want to tell you something. If you've talked to an actual vampire, if one has actually *tasted* your blood, Scrabble just won't chase the nightmares away. And it's a most excellent game.

6

Dracula's Dinner

On the way to school Monday morning, I was in the middle of my vampire story when I noticed Gabe and J.T. exchange a look.

"What?" I said. "Don't you believe me? This guy bit off the head of a *mouse*. I swear."

Gabe kicked away a leaf that had gotten stuck to her hiking boot. "Right, Zach."

"Sure," J.T. said.

They looked at each other again.

"What?" I asked irritably.

Gabe's long hair was pulled back in a thick braid, but blond wisps were already escaping. She blew them out of her eyes. "Look, Zach. We know you've been lying about your weekends uptown. We *know* you have a lousy time. It's pretty obvious. And we let you tell us about all the great things you do with your mom because we *know* you're still freaked out that she doesn't

45

live with you anymore. But enough is enough, okay?"

"Yeah," J.T. said, nodding. He peered at me anxiously. "Okay?"

"Look, you guys," I said. "I admit that maybe I exaggerate about having fun on my up weekends. But this is different."

Gabe sighed again, and blond wisps flew up in the draft. "Zach, you think the truth is like Silly Putty. You're always stretching it and seeing what will happen."

"No, really," I said. "I *swear.* I got on this train, and—"

"What I really want to know is," Gabe interrupted, "did you do that research for our history project? It's due this week."

Gabe and I were partners on a history project in Mr. Potasher's class. Gabe is dyslexic, which means she has a hard time reading because she mixes up letters. She's supersmart, though. So we decided that I would write the presentation and she would take photographs. She's a photography nut. She even has her own darkroom.

I suddenly remembered that I was supposed to look up some topics in my mom's books this weekend. She has all these books on old New York, and I was supposed to come up with a topic.

Gabe stamped her foot, just missing the toe of my sneaker. She was wearing hiking boots, so you can imagine how much *that* would have hurt.

"You didn't do it, did you? I don't believe it. You keep—"

"I *did* think of something. I did!" I said. We stopped outside of school while the inspiration took shape in the Kincaid brain. "We can do our project on the early subway system. We can get into the abandoned City Hall station and take pictures. It will be totally cool!"

"That does sound kind of neat," J.T. said.

Gabe nodded slowly. "I like it. We can go to the station after school today and check it out."

"Yeah, and maybe we'll find some of Zach's vampires," J.T. chortled.

Suddenly, I wished that I'd kept my big mouth shut. What if we *did* see the Undead Express? Sure, then Gabe and J.T. would believe me. But somehow I'd pictured it rolling by while we stood on the platform. It didn't occur to me that it might *stop*. Until now.

After school, we stopped at Gabe's apartment to pick up her Nikon camera. Then we walked down to the station. I showed Gabe and J.T. where I'd pulled the boards aside and we crawled inside and down the dark stairs.

"Wow," Gabe said when we reached the bottom of the stairs. "This is some station."

"Cool," said J.T. "But I wish we brought a flashlight."

Gabe set up the flash on her camera. "This is not just cool," she said as she squeezed off a shot. "This is totally and completely maximum cool. I ride the subway every day, and I never thought about how or when it was built. I bet Mr. Potasher is going to flip over this project."

"I wish I didn't have to work with Amber Sherloff," J.T. said in a mournful voice. "She wants to do our project on the history of garbage collection in New York."

Gabe giggled. Amber's father worked for the sanitation department.

"What's wrong with you, Zach?" she asked, suddenly turning to me. "You seem awfully jumpy."

"Nothing's wrong," I said.

"You keep looking down the tunnel," J.T. said. "Expecting someone?"

"Like a vampire?" Gabe teased.

"You know, I wasn't lying," I said, starting to get angry. "I was telling the truth. Friends should believe each other."

"I believe you met some weirdos," Gabe said. "But vampires? Give me a break." She took another shot.

"Just you wait," I said.

Gabe rolled her round blue eyes.

"I mean it," I said. "Just *wait*. I bet the Undead Express will pull in. All they do is ride around Manhattan. They'll come by. I swear it."

Gabe took a few more pictures. "I think I have enough here," she said. "Where else do you think we should take pictures, Zach? We should find out what the oldest station in Manhattan is." She put the lens cap back on the camera. "Well, that's it for today," she said. "I have to split now. I have to babysit for Piero."

"I have to go, too," J.T. said. "Amber is supposed to call me to discuss the development of the Dumpster."

I wasn't scared anymore. Just angry. They were ignoring me. They didn't believe me!

"I'm not going anywhere," I said. I crossed my arms. "I'm going to *prove* to you that there's a weird train riding around under the city."

Gabe pushed her camera into my hands. "Here. If you see the Undead Express again, take a picture. Okay? But right now, I'm out of here. You know how my mom gets if I'm late."

"And you know how snotty Amber Sherloff can be," J.T. said. "Later, dude."

They climbed the stairs and disappeared. I looked around the empty station. It looked spookier when I was alone. I held onto the camera tighter. It would be worth it all if I could just get a picture of the Undead Express.

I found a crate and sat on it, holding the camera ready to shoot. No way would I let Gabe and J.T. get the better of me. Sure, I had stretched the truth a couple of times. Gabe was right. I *did* think of the truth as Silly Putty. But no matter how much you stretched Silly Putty, it was still Silly Putty. So the truth was still the truth, even if it was stretched a little bit, right?

I heard a noise near the stairs, and I almost jumped to the ceiling. I hoped it wasn't a rat. Then I heard a shuffling, like dragging feet.

My heart started to race and I could feel the blood rushing through my veins. I jumped up, ready to run. There was only one problem. The footsteps were coming from the stairs. I saw a pair of legs coming down. Then a face appeared.

I let out a relieved breath. It was only Harv.

Harv was a homeless guy who lived in the neighborhood. He'd been around as long as I could remember. He usually hung around the takeout Chinese place, since Mr. Wang gave him leftovers if he swept the back alley. During the day he napped in this little park on Broadway.

"Whoa, kid," Harv said. "You gave me a fright."

"Me, too," I said. "What are you doing here, Harv?"

"I come here sometimes when it rains," Harv said. He eyed me. "You got any money, Zach? I didn't have lunch."

"Sure," I said. I dug in the pocket of my jeans and found fifty cents. I put it in his hand.

"Not bad," Harv said. "I can actually pay for my eggroll today. Mr. Wang will pass out. Catch you later, kid."

Harv shuffled back up the stairs, and I sat back down on the crate. Now I could hear the rain dripping through the grating above. I shivered. It was getting chilly and damp down here. A crispy eggroll with hot mustard sounded good.

Maybe it was stupid to wait all afternoon for the Undead Express. How did I know it would roll by? If I left now, I could still get a snack and not spoil my dinner. Or I could drop by Gabe's and see if she'd baked some cookies for Piero. I could think of a *million* things I'd rather be doing than sitting in a dark, damp subway station waiting for vampires to show up.

Just then, I heard the shuffling sound again.

"I don't have any more change, Harv," I called into the darkness. "Promise."

But it wasn't Harv coming out of the gloom. It was someone else. Underneath a hat, chalky skin shone in the gathering darkness. Black eyes glowed in his narrow, mean face. As I watched, he smiled, and saliva dripped off one pointed tooth. It was Sims, the vampire from 1929.

Somehow, I couldn't move. I sat frozen, watching him come closer and closer. He looked hungry.

And there I was. Dinner.

7

Vampire Lessons

Suddenly, behind Sims the red satin lining of a cape unfurled.

"Away!" Valentine ordered. "Go find a rat."

Sims turned to Valentine. "Who do you think you are?" he spat.

Valentine took a threatening step toward him. "I am your leader," he said.

Sims stood his ground. "We want human blood," he said. "You're holding us back."

"You ingrate!" Valentine thundered. "You'd still be losing a fortune on Wall Street if it weren't for me!"

"I should have sold short!" Sims hissed. "Just one more day as a human, and I would have!"

"Right, right," Valentine said impatiently. "Now, if you'll excuse me and my young friend, please."

Sims's eyes darted back to me. He snarled once, then melted back into the darkness.

"Whew," I said. "That was close. For a minute there, I thought I was going to be dinner."

"I told you I'd protect you," Valentine said.

"I remember," I agreed. "But I just can't figure out why."

"I like you, that's why," Valentine said with a smile. He reached behind him and pulled out my backpack from the folds of his cape. "I believe this belongs to you."

"Wow, thanks," I said, taking it.

He sat on the crate next to me. "Why won't you believe me when I say I'll protect you, Zachary?"

"Call me crazy," I said. "But you *are* a vampire. How should I know if you're trustworthy or not?"

"That's rather wise," Valentine said smoothly. "You've already learned vampire lesson number one. Never trust *anyone,* Zachary, not even me. Not even your very closest friends."

"Well, I don't know about *that*," I said. "Gabe and J.T. are my buds. We hang."

"If you'd translate that into English, I'll respond," Valentine said, frowning.

I laughed. "I've known them since I was crawling around eating dust bunnies," I explained.

"So you should trust them," Valentine said.

"Affirmative," I said.

"Ah." Valentine raised an eyebrow. "But tell me, my dear Zachary. Do they trust *you?*"

"Of course they—" I stopped. *Did* Gabe and J.T. trust me? Because if they *did,* why didn't they believe me about the Undead Express?

"I sense some hesitation," Valentine said. "I do believe that you're proving my point."

"Well, they didn't believe me about you," I admitted. "But even I have to admit it's a hard story to swallow."

"But if they're your friends, shouldn't they believe you, no matter what?" Valentine asked.

I didn't say anything. Valentine was right. Gabe and J.T. should know I wouldn't lie to them.

I guess Valentine saw that he'd made me uncomfortable, so he changed the subject. You can't say he didn't have manners, even if his favorite drink was rat blood.

"I see you have a camera," he said. "Are you taking pictures of something special?"

I decided not to tell him about wanting to get evidence of the Undead Express. You never know what might make a vampire touchy.

"I thought this station was kind of neat," I said. "And Gabe and I are doing this history project together on how the subways began. Actually, you gave me the idea the other day."

"Did I? I'm delighted," Valentine said. "Perhaps I can help."

"That would be cool," I said. "I have to do research and stuff. I'm going to write the presentation, and Gabe is going to take the pictures. She just left a little while ago."

"Hmmm," Valentine said. "You say your friend Gabe will take a few pictures, and you will do the writing? That doesn't sound fair. It seems as though she'll get off rather easy."

"Not really," I said defensively. "She's going to develop them and arrange them and everything. And she's going to do research, too. It's just that she's a little slow at reading and writing."

"Well, she's lucky she has a friend she can take advantage of," Valentine said.

"She's not taking advan—"

"I have a splendid idea!" Valentine interrupted. "How would you like to see other abandoned stations?"

"You mean there's more?"

"Oh, yes." Valentine waved a bloodless hand. His eyes glowed. "I can show you wonders. Did you know that at the Waldorf-Astoria Hotel, you used to be able to travel in your own private railway car right into the basement and go upstairs to check in?"

"Cool," I said. "That's like a railway motel."

"And did you know that very wealthy people, like the Vanderbilts, had their own subway stations underneath their mansions? Some of those still exist. *I* can get to them." Valentine leaned closer to me. His breath on my face was like an Arctic wind. "I can show you these things, Zachary. We can make a bargain. I'll show you my world. An enchanted world of eternal night."

"Bargain?" I said. "What do you get from me?"

"Don't worry about that now. I can give you information that no one else will have. You will dazzle your classmates."

"Can Gabe come?" I asked. "She's supposed to take the photographs."

Valentine frowned and moved away. "No. No one else. Only you, Zachary. I trust only you."

"I don't know," I said. "It sounds like it would be cool, but I don't know if my dad would let me."

"Let me tell you about vampire lesson number two, Zachary," Valentine said, his glittering eyes fixed on mine. "You should never have to get permission to really *live*. You must follow the beat of your own blood. No matter what."

I nodded, my eyes glued to his face. I wasn't

57

sure what that meant, but it sounded good to me.

"Now, I must go. My trainmates will be wondering where I've been." Valentine stood up briskly. "Ronnie has organized a singalong of 'I Can't Get No Fulfillment' for our entertainment." He rolled his eyes.

"Satisfaction," I said. "'I Can't Get No Satisfaction.' It's an old song."

"Terrible grammar," Valentine said. "Didn't this Millard Jagger ever go to school?"

"Mick," I said.

Valentine wrapped the cape around himself. "If you want the tour, meet me here tomorrow at this time."

"But how will you know what time it is?" I asked. "I thought there were no clocks on the Undead Express route. Isn't that your big problem?"

Valentine nodded. "I won't know what time it is. But I *will* know when to come to you. Just call me. And I will hear."

"Whatever you say," I said. I had to get a picture of him. I had to show Gabe! I held the camera up and clicked. The light flashed right into Valentine's eyes.

He let out a howl of surprise. Then stepped toward me with a look in his eyes that turned my bones into jelly. Evil flickered in his red glowing eyes. He looked as mean as Sims, and as dangerous.

Then quickly, his face smoothed out, and he smiled. "You surprised me, Zachary. How . . . unexpected. Till tomorrow." I looked down for a second to adjust the camera. When I looked up again, he was gone.

Gabe swished the photo around in the developer. "This will only take a second," she said.

J.T. and I watched as the image took shape. I had come over to Gabe's with the film right after dinner. Finally, I had proof that Valentine existed! I'd make Gabe and J.T. eat their words.

Slowly, the subway station swam into focus. There was the mosaic. There was the tiled wall with CITY HALL spelled out in black and white. There was the iron beam.

But there was no Valentine.

8

Dark Magic

"Vampire, huh?" J.T. scoffed. He ran his hands through his sandy brush cut. "Looks like empty air to me."

Gabe's lips thinned. She peered at the picture. "I already have a picture of the City Hall sign. And this one is out of focus, too."

Suddenly, it all made sense. I looked at my friends in the red glow of the darkroom. "But don't you see?" I cried. "This proves it. This proves Valentine is a vampire!"

"Gee, Zach, run that by me again," J.T. said. "I don't see why." He looked at the picture again. "I don't see *anything*."

"But I aimed the camera right at him!" I said. "And it *didn't take his picture*."

"Zach, you didn't aim it right or something," Gabe said impatiently. "I mean, look. It's out of focus."

"Stop saying that!" I shouted. "I *know* it's out

of focus. I didn't have time to do it perfectly. But I know how to aim a camera, Gabe! You're not the only one who can take pictures!"

She blinked at me and didn't say anything. Even though the red light made her look flushed, I knew that look. I knew her face was pale and her round blue eyes had narrowed. She hated when I yelled.

"Let's go outside," she said. She clipped the photo to a line hanging above the basin to dry it. Then she switched off the light. It was pitch black in the tiny room.

"Come on, J.T.," Gabe said. "Open the door."

I could hear J.T. fumbling with the doorknob. But I wasn't impatient. I was enjoying the darkness. It felt warm and . . . free. I could do anything I wanted in it. I could pick my nose or make a face or stick my tongue out at Gabe. I felt powerful, knowing that. Maybe Valentine wasn't crazy when he talked about the magic of darkness.

"Got it!" J.T. said. The door opened and light flooded in.

Gabe looked at me. "Very mature, Zach," she said angrily. I stuck my tongue back inside my mouth.

Gabe led the way to the kitchen. The Lattanzi kitchen was like ours, except instead of a counter there was a huge metal cart like they used in restaurants. It was full of dishes and pans and baking tins. Gabe's mom, Francesca, was an amazing cook.

Gabe took some juice out of the refrigerator and we sat at the long wooden table. Her notes and photographs were spread out at the end.

"No soda?" J.T. asked, disappointed. His mom is a vegetarian who doesn't believe in sugar. Poor J.T. You can't believe how much he craves cheeseburgers and sodas.

Gabe shook her head. She grabbed a box of chocolate chip cookies and smacked it down on the table. Every cookie must have crumbled into dust. I guessed she was still mad.

"Don't you believe me about Valentine?" I asked her.

"Do I believe he's a vampire?" Gabe asked. "Come *on*, Kincaid."

"Well, do you believe that I met *someone* underground?" I said.

Gabe put her finger in the wet ring the juice bottle had made. She swished it around. "I guess so," she said.

"You *guess* so?"

"Zach, I never know when you're telling the truth," Gabe said. "You're always seeing celebrities at your mom's. Or getting tickets to a game that's sold out. Or your mom is going to take you on a safari in Africa—"

"She is!" I said. "She said she's going to take me!"

Gabe looked at me pityingly. "She wants to take you to Safari World in *Florida*. She told my mom."

Why did Mom and Francesca have to be friends? What a drag.

"Okay, so maybe I exaggerate sometimes," I said. "But Gabe, J.T., I *swear* this is for real."

"Maybe it is, Gabe," J.T. said, munching on a cookie. "I believe in E.T.s. Why not vampires?"

"*Because,*" Gabe said.

"Because it's too scary?" I asked. "Don't be a girl, Gabe."

"No, because it's too *stupid,*" Gabe said. "Don't be a dweeb, Zach. You met some weird guy, like a magician or something, and he's trying to scare you. But you have to blow it up into some story about vampires chasing you. And meanwhile our project is due in three days and you haven't done anything."

"Hey, *I* had the idea!" I said.

"So what?" Gabe said. Then she sighed. "I mean, not so what. It was a great idea. But that's just like you, Zach. You have the idea and then you think that's enough. You don't follow through. I spent two hours in the library this afternoon trying to keep Piero quiet and you sat in a subway station talking to a magician."

"I took the picture," I pointed out.

"It's out of focus," Gabe said.

Now I really got mad. "You have a lot of nerve, Lattanzi, when I'm the one who has the hardest job," I said. "All you have to do is take pictures. I have to write the presentation. I let you do the photographs because you're dyslexic. You're the one who's taking advantage of *me*."

Gabe's neck had red splotches on it. "I didn't know you thought that," she said.

"Well, I do!" I said. I never had before, but I did right then.

J.T. raised his eyebrows and looked back and forth from Gabe to me. He munched on his cookie. It was the only sound in the loft.

"Well, maybe we shouldn't be partners, then," Gabe said, her voice shaking. "I'll just tell Mr. Potasher that I have my own project."

"Fine with me," I said, shrugging.

"Here," she said, shoving the photographs at me. "You can have the ones I took already."

I pushed them back at her. A little voice was in my head, saying *do it*. It was like I was looking down on Gabe and J.T. Like I wasn't part of them anymore. I was better than they were because I had seen something they never would.

"Take them," I said. "I don't need them. I'll do a better job without them."

Tears sprang to Gabe's eyes. She grabbed the photos and ripped them up. J.T. stopped chewing, shocked.

"Fine!" she said. "I don't want them, either!"

Gabe looked away and took a sip of juice. I knew she didn't want me to see that she'd almost started to cry. I had really hurt her feelings. But that same little voice in my head stopped me from apologizing. *Why should I?* That feeling I'd had in the closet came back to me, the feeling of power. I could feel blood swishing through my veins, beating against my skin. It was *Valentine's* power I felt. The power of the night.

And I knew I had to find the heart of that power. I knew where I had to go.

"I knew you would call," Valentine said.

I sat next to him on the crate. "I had to."

"Yes, Zachary. You had to." He looked at me, with a twinkle in his eye. "And did you get *permission?*"

"I told my dad I was sleeping at J.T.'s house," I said.

"Good," Valentine said. "You are learning,

Zachary. Learning that the secret to life is to act on your own. To trust yourself. To follow the beat of your own blood." He stood up and unfurled his cape. "Now. Let us begin."

Then Valentine took me on a journey. It was a gray world and full of shadows. But he walked into the shadows and I followed him, and I wasn't afraid. We walked through tunnels and passageways without a flashlight. But we didn't need one. I saw everything. Suddenly, I could see as clearly in the dark as I could in bright sunlight. And I realized that sunlight *wasn't* the way to see anything. It was too harsh. It made you miss things.

We came out in magnificent tiled rooms with mosaics of wonderful colors. I saw gilded columns and tiles in deep maroons and ruby reds. There was an incredible world underneath my city, and I'd never even known.

I had borrowed Dad's camera, and I got lots of pictures—in focus. Valentine waited patiently while I set up shots and explored the stations. He told me facts and I scribbled them down. This was going to be the greatest project in the class, and it was all because I trusted Valentine. It was the best decision I'd ever made.

The last station was the most incredible of all. It had a ceiling that curved into a dome over our heads. Painted on the ceiling was an amazing scene in deep colors of a train going through a weird landscape of twisted trees and a blood-red setting sun. Every column glittered with gold paint. The floor was made of creamy marble. The whole station seemed to glow. But the strangest thing of all was that it was *clean*. All the other stations seemed to have centuries of grime over everything.

I circled around, wondering where to shoot first. "Wow," I said. "Whose station was this?"

"Mine," Valentine said. "It was below my office. The building is gone now. I heard them above me, tearing it down." He looked around. "But this remains. I designed it. I created it. It's all mine."

"It's beautiful," I said.

He smiled. His teeth didn't bother me at all anymore. "Maximum cool?"

"Off the scale," I said. "Totally." I raised the camera, but he put a hand over it.

"No, Zachary. No pictures. This is just for you. If someone sees the pictures, they may look for this place. And I want it to remain like this. Perfect. Beautiful."

"Okay," I said, lowering the camera. "No sweat. I have plenty of stuff already. I—"

"Shhh." Valentine held up a hand to stop me.

"Listen. Can you hear them?"

"Hear who?" I whispered. "Rats?" I hoped Valentine wasn't ready for his dinner.

"People," he said. "Above us. Is it dark now, Zachary?"

I looked at my watch. "Yes," I said.

"I thought so." Valentine closed his eyes. "I see them walking. Enjoying the night air. Heading to a restaurant for dinner, or to a concert. Walking home from work. Strolling under the stars. Living and breathing, alive in the night. Do you hear the beating of their hearts?"

"Not really," I said. "But I'll take your word for it."

"I want to walk among them, Zachary. I want to smell the night air." Valentine opened his eyes. "Take me to them. Show me the way."

"Uh, wait a second," I said, stalling. I hadn't expected this. Being underground with Valentine was one thing. But I couldn't take him aboveground. Anything could happen. He was a vampire!

"What about our bargain?" Valentine asked.

"Bargain? What bargain?" I said, stalling.

"I showed you my world," Valentine said, waving his hand. "And now you will show me yours."

"But I never made that bargain!" I exclaimed.

"You never said the part about taking you above-ground!"

"But you accepted the bargain, nevertheless," Valentine said. "You heard what you wanted to hear." His gaze fixed on mine.

I stared into his eyes. I felt drawn down into a pool of dark water. I wanted to yawn, but I couldn't. I felt so sleepy and warm. There was a medallion around his neck, and the gold glinted at me.

"Zachary, I won't bite anything," Valentine said soothingly. "Not a rat, not a dog. You will be with me every step. Let me show you why the night is magic. Let me see the stars again. Will you take me?"

This time, I didn't hesitate. I said, "Yes."

9

The Nightwalk

We walked back through the twisting tunnels, crawled through an opening, and came back in the City Hall station.

Valentine gazed hungrily at the stairs. "At last," he said.

I climbed the steps with Valentine on my heels. I pushed apart the boards and squeezed through. I didn't know if Valentine would make it, but he slipped through like a shadow.

He stood, straight and tall, looking up at the stars. He took deep breaths of the cool night air. For a minute, he staggered, and I thought he would fall down. Behind him a shadow loomed, then retreated. A rat? I didn't want to find out.

"Are you okay?" I asked.

Valentine turned to me. From the light of the moon, I could see his pale face clearly. Something was glittering on his cheeks. It couldn't be tears, though. I know as well as anybody that vampires don't cry.

"I've waited so long," he said.

"Well, come on then," I said. "There's a lot to see."

If you ever want a truly insane experience, try showing your town to somebody who hasn't seen it in a hundred years. It's pretty wild. Valentine had never seen a helicopter or a skyscraper. When we passed the Woolworth Building, he couldn't believe how tall it was. I think it's maybe fifty floors. I turned him around to face the World Trade Center, which is over a hundred floors, and he let out a scream.

How do you like that? I scared a vampire.

It was early enough at night that people who worked late were leaving their offices and heading home. We passed a woman in a miniskirt, and I had to convince Valentine she wasn't wearing her underwear.

We walked sixty blocks up Broadway to Herald Square. That's about three miles, total. Valentine never got tired. Finally, I had to stop and rest, so I pulled him into a fast-food place. He couldn't believe you could order a hamburger and get it in three minutes wrapped in paper with a container of fries. But when he gave it a good sniff, he said it didn't smell like meat. He's probably right.

I took Valentine over to the East Side to show him the old brownstones. I thought it would be nice for him to see something familiar, but he wasn't really interested. He wanted to see more big buildings, so we walked back across to Fifth Avenue.

"It's marvelous," he said. He pointed up the avenue with his cane. "Commerce. Industry. Wealth. New York has surpassed my expectations."

"I don't know," I said. "I like downtown better, where the buildings are smaller. It's more homey."

"Progress, Zachary," Valentine said, staring up at the Empire State Building. "Never let anything stand in its way. Knock down the old, build the new."

"I guess," I said. I decided then and there not to tell Valentine that my dad was head of the Save Our Historical Buildings committee.

We walked all night. After midnight, there were fewer and fewer people on the streets. We made no sound on the concrete sidewalks. I was wearing sneakers, and Valentine barely seemed to touch the ground. I never heard his footsteps. It was like being invisible.

We ended up taking the subway—the *real* subway—back downtown. We got off at Canal Street and walked down to the City Hall station. The sky was becoming a little lighter, and I noticed Valentine was getting weak.

When we got to the secret entrance, he turned to me.

"Thank you, Zachary," he said with a little bow.

"You're welcome," I replied politely. Then I suddenly realized something. "Hey," I said. "Once I told you that it was night, you could have done this yourself. You didn't need me. Why did you ask me to come?"

His eyes twinkled. "I wanted the company."

Valentine drew his cape around himself and oozed through the boards. How did he *do* it? I turned around and started toward home. Nobody was on the street. If Mom or Dad found out I was walking on Broadway this late, I'd be in huge trouble. It seemed silly to worry about that kind of stuff after walking around New York with a vampire, though.

I had only gone about three blocks when I felt a cold hand on my shoulder. I gave a start, but it was Valentine. I hadn't heard him come up.

"I'm glad I found you," he said. "Something has happened."

"What?" I asked nervously. If it was possible for Valentine to look even more pale, he did.

"It's Sims," he said. "He's missing."

"Missing?"

Valentine nodded. "I think he may have followed us, Zachary."

Suddenly, I remembered the shadow at the City Hall station. How it had loomed, and then retreated. That had been no rat! Or rather, it *had.*

"Come," Valentine said urgently. "It may already be too late."

"Too late?" I gulped. "You mean . . ."

"He's hungry," Valentine said. *"We must find him, Zachary."*

Valentine decided that Sims wouldn't go uptown. He was a Wall Street kind of guy. Maybe he would break into the New York Stock Exchange so he could sell short.

By the way, remind me to find out what selling short *is.* Somehow I don't think it has anything to do with being behind the underwear counter at Macy's.

We walked all over the Wall Street area. We prowled in alleys and peeked in Dumpsters. We crept through Battery Park and peered beneath benches. It was not the most fun I've ever had.

Valentine had started to breathe heavily. Then he almost fell.

"I'm getting weaker, Zachary," he said. "Dawn is approaching."

"We'd better get back," I said. "Maybe Sims will be there. He'll be getting weaker, too."

"Unless he's found somewhere to hide," said Valentine. "Is there a building nearby that he could get inside? A basement where no one would find him?"

"I don't know," I said.

"A cemetery?" Valentine asked. He gripped my arm so hard it hurt. "He could climb into a vault."

"There's no cemetery down here," I said. "Except for the graveyard at Trinity Church—"

"That must be it!" Valentine gasped. "We've got to go there!"

I gulped. "Now?" Wandering around a graveyard with a vampire wasn't exactly my idea of a good time.

"Yes, before it's too late!" Valentine said.

We hurried along the deserted streets. When we reached the church, we climbed over the iron fence and dropped onto the grass. The gravestones shone in the pale light. Famous people are buried here, like Alexander Hamilton and Robert Fulton. I sure didn't feel like waking them up.

"We need to find a crypt," Valentine whispered.

"Valentine—" I said. But I stopped. Actually, I think my *heart* might have stopped for a moment. Sims had risen behind a gravestone. Blood dripped down his chin.

"Catch him!" Valentine shouted.

Excuse me?

"Hurry!" Valentine said. He vaulted over the stone and crashed down on Sims. All I heard was hissing and snarling.

By the time I ran around the stone, Valentine was sitting on top of Sims. "You have no choice," he said, his face inches away from Sims's. "I'm ordering you to return."

Sims turned his head from side to side. "Never! I haven't tasted human blood yet! Doesn't anyone work late on Wall Street anymore?"

"Sims, dawn is coming," Valentine said urgently. "We must go."

"No," he snarled. "I can find a place to rest."

"There is no place to rest. Not for us," Valentine said. He sounded tired. "Don't you understand that yet? Now come."

He got off Sims. To my surprise, Sims didn't argue. He just stood up. Suddenly, he seemed tired, too.

"Take us back, Zachary," Valentine said wearily. He looked terrible.

I led them back toward the station. I left them at the end of a nearby vacant lot. When I turned back, I could just make them out as they picked their way through the trash toward the entrance.

The sky was lighter, but I couldn't see the sun yet. As I walked back home, I saw the rosy light begin to touch the stones of the building. I didn't feel tired at all. Even though we had a close call with Sims, it had been the best night of my life.

I pushed open the door of the loft and tiptoed inside. I closed it, wincing when it squeaked a little bit.

When I turned around, I saw Dad sitting at the kitchen table with a cup of coffee. He was unshaven and looked like a total wreck.

I had just walked through the night with a vampire, but I had a feeling my troubles were only beginning.

10

The Beat of Your Own Blood

"Where have you been, Zachary?" Dad asked. His voice was very quiet. It was not a good sign.

"I told you," I said nervously. "I spent the night at—"

"Do not lie to me!" Dad suddenly yelled. From the dark circles under his eyes I could tell he'd been up all night. "I know that you were not at J.T.'s," he continued in a softer voice. "Gabe called here looking for you, and I told her you were at J.T.'s. She asked if you were going with J.T. to his brother's piano recital. I said I didn't know, but then I called the Heffernans to find out. I wanted to make sure you had a clean shirt with you."

J.T.'s brother Max went to Juilliard, which is a famous music school uptown. I couldn't go to a recital there in jeans and a T-shirt. Whoops.

"I'm asking you again, Zachary," Dad said. "Where were you?"

I decided to tell the truth. Not the *whole* truth, of course. Just some of it.

"I was with Valentine," I said. "The new friend I met on the subway. He's a magician. We rode around on the subway, and then we sat in a cafeteria all night."

"Do you mean to tell me that you spent the whole night roaming around New York City?" Dad roared. "With someone you met on the *subway*?"

"It was fun," I said defiantly. "Valentine wanted to show me the night. How mysterious it is. And the reason I didn't ask you was, well, you shouldn't need to ask permission to truly live. The secret of life," I continued, "is to follow the beat of your own blood."

Dad looked worried. "Where are you getting this stuff, Zach?"

I shrugged. I realized that maybe I'd gone a little too far.

"From your new friend?" Dad asked.

I felt strange, as though part of me was still roaming free in the dark. Dad seemed so far away. "From the magic of the night," I whispered.

Now Dad looked scared. "You're never going to see that guy again, Zach. Do you hear me?"

"I hear you," I said. But only part of me did.

The other part of me was listening to the harsh clang of garbage cans. The world was waking up outside. I thought how stupid it was to live your life in the daytime, to sleep while the moon and stars roamed the sky. It seemed so foolish to waste the night.

I got to take the morning off, since I'd been up all night. But Dad woke me up for lunch and then sent me to school. He still looked worried and upset. He said that maybe I *should* live uptown, where the security was better. But he wasn't going to tell my mother about this . . . yet. If I didn't get back to normal, he'd have to.

Normal? What was so great about that?

I sat through my afternoon classes without really listening. I was trying to figure out how I could get out of the house in the next few days. I was grounded, of course. But I wasn't going to let that stop me.

Gabe and J.T. caught up to me as I put on my jacket after school.

"What happened?" Gabe asked me, wide-eyed.

"Where were you?" J.T. asked at the same time.

"Thanks for nothing, you guys," I said. "I'm grounded. You could have covered for me."

"How could we cover for you if we didn't know what was going on?" Gabe asked.

"Besides, you should have told *someone* where you were going," J.T. said. "What if something bad had happened to you?"

"Don't be a wimp," I said. "You should come with us next time."

"Who is us?" Gabe asked.

"Me and Valentine," I said.

Gabe chewed on the end of her braid. I hadn't seen her do that since she was seven. "You're not going to do it *again,* are you?"

"Why not?" I said. "Valentine has this great saying. You shouldn't have to get permission to truly live. That's what our parents do to us. We have to ask them permission to live."

Gabe and J.T. exchanged a worried glance. "Are you listening to this vampire now?" J.T. asked. He hitched up his pants nervously. His mom always buys him clothes that are a little too big.

"I thought you said he wasn't a vampire," I retorted. "So why do you look so worried?"

"Well, he *says* he's a vampire," Gabe said. "So he's definitely strange. And scary. Zach, this is serious stuff. This guy could be dangerous."

"Yeah, Zach," J.T. said. "What's going on with you, anyway? You're acting so weird."

"I am not," I said. "I'm doing cool stuff, and you guys can't handle it. You're jealous."

"Right," Gabe said sarcastically. "I always wanted Dracula for my very best friend."

"Listen, I have to go," I said. "Thanks to you guys, I have to go straight home after school."

"I have to go, too," Gabe mumbled. "I have a lot of work to do on my project. It's due tomorrow."

"So's mine," I said. "I'm going to knock everyone's socks off with the pictures I got last night. Just you wait."

I left Gabe and J.T. standing on the corner.

I walked over to Hudson Street to drop off my film. The guy told me it would *definitely* be done tomorrow morning. That meant I'd have time to arrange the slides in my first period study hall. Wait until Gabe found out I got an A without her. She'd freak. I couldn't wait to see her face!

On the way home, I stopped off at Mr. Wang's takeout place. A couple of his crispy eggrolls would hold me over until dinner. I found him standing in the doorway, frowning.

"What's happening, Mr. Wang?" I greeted him.

"Hello, Zach," he said. "Nothing much. But have you seen Harvey today?"

"Harv? No," I said. "Usually I see him on the

way to school, but I was late this morning. Can I have two shrimp rolls, please?"

Mr. Wang put the rolls in a bag with some hot mustard. He rang up the sale. "Every day, three o'clock, Harvey is here for hot-and-sour soup. Rain or shine. But not today."

I took the bag of eggrolls.

"Very strange," Mr. Wang said. He handed me my change.

"Yeah. Well—"

"This morning, I was going to the produce market for my vegetables. Near dawn," Mr. Wang said. "I saw him with two tall men. They were in that vacant lot, over by Broadway. Something about those two men bothered me. Very strange."

Strange doesn't cover it, Mr. Wang.

Harv! I whirled around. I started to run.

"Zach! Your eggrolls!" Mr. Wang yelled after me.

I clattered down the stairs of the City Hall station. Panting, I stood on the edge of the platform.

"Valentine!" I screamed. "Where are you?"

But my words just echoed down the long, dark tunnel.

11

What Are Best Friends For?

Dad was still upset, and he tried to ask me more about Valentine at dinner. But I didn't say much. I was too busy thinking. I decided I was being completely paranoid about Harv.

The two men Mr. Wang was talking about could have been anybody. Harv had plenty of pals, guys who lived in the park or in abandoned buildings. Harv had probably decided to get lost for a few days.

I had something more important to worry about—my project. I didn't have the slides yet, but I could remember almost every shot I took. I wrote my presentation around the pictures. It was too bad I didn't have Gabe's research, but I had my notes from Valentine's talk. Mr. Potasher would be so blown away by the slides he wouldn't even pay attention to what I was saying, anyway.

When night fell, I was restless. I went into

my room and opened the window all the way. I wanted to let in as much of the night as I could. I leaned on the sill and breathed in the air. It was like someone—or something—was out there, calling to me.

"Soon," I whispered to the dark streets below. "Soon . . ."

The next morning, I waited until I heard the Lattanzi door shut across the hall. I knew Gabe was standing in the hall. We always walked to school together. I knew she was hesitating, wondering whether to knock on our door. But after a minute, she went down the stairs.

Good. She'd just lecture me again. I waited another few minutes so I wouldn't run into her. Then I had to run to Hudson Street to pick up my slides. I made it to school seconds before the bell rang.

For first period study hall, Mrs. Nowicki marched us all to the library, where we split up and sat at tables. We got to do whatever we wanted, read a book for fun, or do homework. Usually I'd read a few pages and pass notes to Gabe and J.T. Today, I had work to do.

I found a place on a windowseat, behind a dull brown velvet curtain, away from everyone else. I opened the envelope and took out the slide sheet.

I held it up to the light. Every single slide was black!

The curtain moved, and I quickly dropped the slides into my lap. J.T.'s freckled face appeared around the curtain.

"Hey," he said in a friendly voice. "How's it going?"

You've got to hand it to the guy. It didn't take much for him to want to make up. Gabe and I laugh about it sometimes, in a nice way. When we were younger and would get into a terrific fight over Monopoly or something, J.T. would stamp off home, saying he'd never speak to us again. Within a half hour, he'd be at your door with a bagful of these horrible granola brownies from his mom, wanting to make up. J.T. didn't know what a grudge *was*.

Now Gabe—she was the champ. She could stay mad at you for *days*.

"It's going okay," I said. I tucked the slides underneath my notebook. But that only drew J.T.'s attention to them.

"How'd your slides come out? Are they as fabuloso as you said?"

"Better," I said. If I told J.T. none of the slides had come out, he'd tell Gabe. Then she'd laugh in my face. "I'm kind of busy, J.T.," I said.

His face fell. "Oh. Okay. Well. Catch you later." His face disappeared around the curtain. I took out the slides and looked at them again. What had happened? I could understand not being able to photograph a vampire, but a subway station?

Then I realized what happened. I groaned out loud, then tried to cover it up with a cough.

I knew why the slides were black. It had nothing to do with the supernatural. I'd left the lens cap on.

"Excellent, Gabrielle," Mr. Potasher said. "The graphic approach was very imaginative. And your photography is quite impressive."

"Thanks, Mr. Potasher," Gabe said. Her face glowed. She turned to pack up her stuff.

"The information about the Chrysler Building was fascinating," Mr. Potasher went on. "You must have spent a lot of time on this."

"I guess so," Gabe said modestly. She caught my eye and grinned. I looked away.

Mr. Potasher looked at the class list. "Now can we hear from . . . Zach Kincaid?"

Can I just stop here a minute? I want to ask something. Why is it that when you've spent hours and hours on a project, you don't get called on? And when you haven't even looked *up* your topic in the card catalog, the teacher calls your name?

Just wondering.

I had spent my lunch hour Xeroxing these awful photographs of subway stations that I found in an ancient book on the history of New York City. They came out terrible, and I knew I'd get a C or even a D if I based my presentation on them. There was nothing else to do but postpone. I'd have to somehow convince Dad to let me out this afternoon, and then I'd find Valentine and take more pictures.

I stood up. "I'm sorry, Mr. Potasher. But I'm not prepared. Can I have until tomorrow?"

"You're aware, Zach, that this means you will drop a grade?"

"Yes, Mr. Potasher." At least it would be from an A to a B. *If* I could get those photos.

Mr. Potasher drew his lips together in that way he does when he's displeased. "Very well, Zach. Next, Allison Tulchin?"

Gabe gave me a puzzled glance. I turned my attention to the fascinating Allison Tulchin and her discussion of the history of department stores.

I was almost dozing during last period in

Mrs. Nowicki's English class when Mick the Mixmaster leaned over and poked me.

"They still haven't fixed the clock, Kincaid," he said. "What do you say we go for round two?"

"What do you mean, *we?*" I muttered.

"I'll back you up, buddy," the Mixmaster promised. "Just go for it."

"Forget it," I said. I looked down at my book again. But then I thought of something. If I got out of school early, I would have time to photograph two or three stations before Dad started to wonder where I was. He was teaching today, and he'd call home at four to make sure I was there. Maybe I'd run into Valentine again.

I raised my hand. "Uh, Mrs. Nowicki?"

"Yes, Zachary?" She put her finger in the book to mark her place, but I could tell she wasn't really listening to me.

"The clock stopped again," I said. "It's one minute past three."

"It is?"

I waited for the Mixmaster to say, *Absolutely, Mrs. Nowicki,* but he sat there like a dumb ox. I should have figured.

Then, Mrs. Nowicki did something that sent a chill right to my heart. She reached into her desk drawer and took out a small travel clock. Slowly, her eyes rose to meet mine.

"I think there's some hanky-panky going on," she said. "And wait one moment here. Zach, did you lie to me last week about the time?"

The class fell silent.

"He did, Mrs. Nowicki," Allison Tulchin piped up. Janie Russo poked her in her back with her pen. "But we didn't realize it until we got outside," she said quickly.

Mrs. Nowicki sighed. "I don't like this, Mr. Kincaid. It looks like a certain young man will be sitting in detention today."

"Is it me?" I asked.

"And I'll tell Mr. Gonzaga to keep an eye on the clock," Mrs. Nowicki said firmly.

So my plan hit a major snag. But you can't struggle against fate. When the bell rang, I went to the room where detention was being held. But first, I called Dad at Cooper Union and told him. Let me tell you, he did not take the news well.

I sat and tried to do homework, but it was hard to concentrate. The hands of the clock moved v-e-r-y slowly. My stomach growled, and I thought of shrimp rolls at Mr. Wang's. But that made me think of Harv, so I tried to do homework again.

Suddenly, I heard a hiss. I was sitting in the

very last seat, and I looked into the hall. J.T. was there.

"I just wanted to tell you not to worry," J.T. said in a loud whisper. "I told Gabe your slides came out all black—"

"How did you know?"

"I saw them, Zach," J.T. said. "You didn't hide them quick enough. Anyway, Gabe is going to photograph the City Hall station again. She even destroyed her negatives when she was mad, and she feels guilty. So you can use the pictures tomorrow for your presentation."

"Wait," I said. "Are you saying that Gabe is doing me a *favor?*"

J.T. shrugged. "What are best friends for? Catch you later." J.T. waved and moved off.

I stared straight ahead. I was thinking about Harv again. And Sims with his bloody teeth. Cold dread started somewhere around my toes and inched up my body until it crawled out the ends of my hair.

Gabe would be alone in the City Hall station with a bunch of vampires. And it was all my fault!

12

The Joke's on Me

You'd be surprised what fake barfing can do for you under the right circumstances. Mr. Gonzaga looked like he was going to lose it himself. Especially when I told him I'd eaten a tuna fish burrito for lunch.

I got out of detention and ran all the way to J.T.'s. His parents weren't home from work yet, and he was playing a computer game.

"What's the matter?" he asked. "Vampires chasing you?"

"No," I said, panting. "But they might be chasing Gabe."

Quickly, I explained about my nightwalk. I told J.T. how Sims craved human blood. J.T. looked fascinated, as though he was watching a horror movie. But after I was through, he seemed to bump back down into real life.

"Are you trying to play a trick on me?" he asked suspiciously. "Is Gabe in on this?"

"J.T., I'm straight. I double swear," I said. "All I want you to do is cover for me. Dad thinks I'm in detention, and he gets home around five. If I'm not back by then, will you call and tell him I got sick and you brought me here? Tell him I'm asleep, or barfing, and can't come to the phone."

"You must be crazy," J.T. said. "First of all, why would your dad believe me? He knows you used me before to stay out all night."

"That's *why* he would believe you," I said. "You could have gotten in trouble because of me. Why would you cover for me now?"

"Right," J.T. said. "Hey, wait. Since that's true, why *would* I cover for you?"

"Because of Gabe," I said. "She's in danger."

J.T. brushed his hair straight up, making it look sillier than ever. "Is this vampire stuff really real, Zach? Double swear on the memory of Algernon."

Algernon had been Gabe's dog, a truly dumb springer spaniel. Last summer, when Gabe's family went to Florida, J.T. and I took turns watching him. One day when we were walking him, he'd got loose from his leash and ran away. Gabe had made the leash herself out of braided leather, and we were always telling her to buy a decent one. We kept telling her it was getting frayed. Have I mentioned that she's stubborn?

J.T. and I had split up to find Algernon. We both came around the block on White Street from different ends and saw it happen. Algernon got hit by a car. He flew in the air and landed on the sidewalk. The car kept going.

He was still alive when we got to him. He was whimpering, and his big brown eyes rolled up at us, saying *save me*. It was the most awful thing I'd ever seen. We picked him up and walked him to the animal hospital on West Broadway, but he died. We couldn't stand Gabe knowing the story. It wasn't that we were afraid she'd blame us. We were afraid she'd blame herself because of the frayed leash. We told her that Algernon had died in his sleep. He was pretty old.

It was our deepest, darkest secret.

I looked J.T. right in the eye. "I double swear on the memory of Algernon," I said.

J.T. let out a shaky breath. I realized he'd been holding it. "Gosh," he said. Suddenly he looked really scared. "Vampires!"

"That's what I've been trying to tell you," I said. "So will you do it?"

"I'll do it," J.T. said. His freckles stood out from his white face. "If it gets to be five and we're not back, I'll call from a pay phone somewhere."

94

"We? A pay phone? What do you mean?"

J.T. looked grim. "I'm coming with you."

J.T. stuck close to me as we inched down the stairs at the City Hall station. We stopped at the bottom until our eyes got used to the darkness.

"Do you see anyone—I mean, any, uh, *thing?*" he whispered.

I shook my head. "Remember what I told you," I said. "You don't have to worry about Valentine. He'll protect us. But be careful of the others."

"If we see any of them, we run, right?" J.T. asked hopefully.

"Definitely," I said.

"I've been thinking, Zach," J.T. said as he followed close on my heels. "Remember the story you told about being on the Undead Express?"

"What about it?" I asked. I moved toward the corner where the crates were.

"Remember, you said that a vampire touched the blood on your leg and then drank it? Well, I remember from reading about vampires that once they taste your blood, they're sort of . . . in you. I know the vampire only got a teeny taste. But what if that's why you've been acting so weird lately?"

I stopped, and J.T. bumped into me. I wanted to tell him that his theory was the stupidest

95

thing I'd ever heard. But maybe he was right. I'd felt so strange at night. Hot and restless and wanting to be free, outside and roaming. Maybe it *did* have to do with a vampire tasting my blood.

Something rustled in the corner, and J.T. jumped back and landed on my foot.

"Ow!" I said.

"Shhh," J.T. said. "I think there's someone over there."

We inched forward toward the long shadows. Suddenly, a hand reached over a crate. J.T. grabbed the hem of my jacket as a head followed. "Harv!" I exclaimed. "Where have you been? Mr. Wang is looking everywhere for you."

"Sorry," Harv said in his raspy voice. "Just taking a break. Even guys like me need a vacation once in a while." He eased himself up on the crate.

We walked over to him. "Listen, we were wondering," I said. "Have you seen our friend Gabe? You know, the girl with the blond hair? She wears it in a braid mostly."

Harv licked his lips. "I know her. Have I seen her? Mmm. Let me think . . ."

Over Harv's shoulder, I saw a dead rat. J.T. must have seen it, too. "Ewwww," he said, screwing up his face.

The rat looked kind of . . . flat, as though all the stuffing was out of it. Or all the blood. "Harv," I said in a shaky voice, "um, where *have* you been the past couple of days?"

"Around," Harv said. He smiled. His eyeteeth had turned into fangs. They were red. "Care to join me for a bite?" he asked.

J.T. screamed and backed up, pulling me with him. I kept the iron pillar between me and Harv. "Where's Gabe?" I asked, trying to sound brave. "You *have* seen her, haven't you?"

"Valentine took her for a ride," Harv said. "On the Undead Express."

"It's okay, J.T.," I said. "At least she's with Valentine. He'll protect her."

Harv snorted. "Protect her?"

I nodded nervously. "He doesn't suck the blood of humans," I said.

Harv smiled. "Who told you *that?*" he asked.

"Valentine," I said uneasily.

"And you believed him?"

Harv threw back his head and laughed, his bloody teeth glinting through the gloom.

13

A Terrible Bargain

I felt J.T. tug the back of my jacket. "Come on, Zach. Let's get out of here."

But I couldn't move. Could Valentine really have lied to me? Could he have betrayed me?

"Wait," I muttered. "I want to ask—"

But suddenly, Harv rose up. He snarled, and his eyes glowed, red and hot.

"Come *on*, Zach!" J.T. yanked my jacket harder, and I stumbled backward as Harv came after us. My feet didn't seem to be able to move, but J.T. kept pulling me until I was jerked into a run.

We raced across the platform and toward the stairs. Harv was snuffling and snarling and roaring behind us. His hands snatched at our jackets. From the shadow in front of us it looked as though we were being chased by an enormous bat.

We got to the stairs and raced up, barely

touching the ground by now. Harv fell on one knee and howled in frustration. But he was up again and faster than before, certainly faster than the *old* Harv could have been.

I reached the top step and started to push aside the boards.

"Zach!" J.T. screamed.

I turned and saw that Harv had J.T. by the collar. His mouth was open and his teeth glinted at me, poised over J.T.'s neck.

Quickly, I pulled apart the boards. A shaft of sunlight flooded through the opening, hitting Harv in the face.

"*Yeeeoooooowww!*" Harv clutched his face and fell backward into the shadows. That gave J.T. a chance to sprint up toward me. I pushed him through the opening and then squeezed through.

We collapsed on the ground, panting. That had been close. *Too* close.

"I don't believe this is happening," J.T. panted.

"You were pretty good down there," I told him. "I couldn't move. You saved me."

"And you saved *me*," J.T. said. "But I never want to do that again."

As soon as the words left his mouth, J.T. looked at me. I stared back at him. We both knew that we *did* have to do it again. For Gabe.

For a second, I thought J.T. was going to back out. And you know something? I wouldn't blame him a bit. It wasn't *his* fault that Gabe had been kidnapped by a vampire. She might even *be* a vampire herself by now.

"You don't have to come," I told him. "This whole thing is my fault. If I hadn't told you and Gabe lies all the time, you would have believed me about the vampires. That's number one. And if I hadn't been so mean to Gabe, she wouldn't have torn up those pictures *and* the negatives."

"And if we weren't best friends, she wouldn't have gone to take *more* pictures," J.T. said. "And if we didn't care, we wouldn't try to save her. But here we are." He stood up and tugged up his pants. "Where to now? Where would Valentine take Gabe?"

"I think I have an idea," I said.

"Great!" J.T. said. He tried to look brave but failed. His expression was probably like mine. I was just as terrified as he was. Maybe more. I knew more than he did.

"There's only one problem," I said. "We have to go back down there."

I eased the boards apart quietly. Then I tiptoed halfway down the stairs. J.T. waited outside. We decided that if I shouted, he should open the boards and let the sun in. Harv would be weakened by his exposure to the light for at least a few minutes. But he wouldn't be dead.

I tiptoed down a few steps. Then I heard a sound that made my heart thump with relief.

Snoring.

Harv had fallen asleep. He was stretched out behind the crates. The only thing visible were his feet in those dirty running shoes he wore.

I hurried quietly back upstairs. "All clear," I said softly. "He's asleep. But be *very* quiet."

J.T. nodded and followed me back inside. We tiptoed down the staircase and moved noiselessly across the platform. Once, Harv stirred, and J.T. stifled a squeak. We moved on.

We made our way along the platform and jumped down onto the tracks. I knew that no trains were going to come through, and I was gambling that the Undead Express was stopped where we were headed. You'd think that once a vampire has chased you through a dark abandoned subway station you'd be ready for anything. But it was almost as scary to walk down subway tracks in a dark tunnel. Especially when I wasn't quite sure I remembered the way. If J.T. had asked me one more time if we were getting close, I would have bopped him in the nose.

Finally, we crawled through a passage and came to a tunnel that I recognized. There was a faint, flickering light at the end of it. J.T. looked at me, and I nodded. I saw him swallow.

We walked down the tracks. When we came through the end of the tunnel, we saw the Undead Express drawn up to the platform of Valentine's private station. Candles lit up the domed ceiling and the gilded columns. The light flickered over the dead-white faces of the vampires and turned the lining of Valentine's cape into fire.

And it shone on the pale, frightened face of Gabe.

J.T. let out a gasp. The vampires' heads swiveled toward us.

Valentine smiled and extended an arm. "Ah, gentlemen. We've been expecting you."

We climbed up on the platform and walked toward them. Valentine was standing next to Gabe. Sims was at the head of the crowd of vampires. It looked like we had interrupted something. What was going on?

"Valentine, please let her go," I said. "Take me instead."

Sims let out a harsh laugh. "We don't bargain with the living. Tell me, boy, why should we let *any* of you go?"

"How could you do this to me?" I asked Valentine. "You told me you didn't go after humans. You told me you would protect me."

"I'm a vampire, Zachary," Valentine said smoothly. "Evil is my nature."

I looked at his narrow, pale face. How could I have trusted him?

"But I told you not to trust anyone," Valentine said. "Not even me. And you had a clue."

"A clue?" I asked.

"I told you that I had started this line of vampires," Valentine said. "That I had ushered them into the world of the night. How could I have done that without tasting human blood?"

"That's right," I said. "I'm so stupid!"

"No," Valentine said softly. "You heard what you wanted to hear."

"Enough of this talk," Sims said. He took a step toward Gabe. "She's so . . . healthy."

"Wait a second," Ronnie said. He fingered the fringe on his vest nervously. "I thought we agreed. This is a democracy, man. We're going to draw lots for her, remember?"

"But we have two more now," Sims said. "And I'm the one who found her."

"And *I* am the one who stopped you from destroying the plan!" Valentine thundered. "Or are all of you forgetting what we discussed?"

103

The vampires all looked kind of sheepish. Ronnie looked at his sandaled feet. Pearl played with her ribbons. Dwayne tugged on an eyebrow.

"Listen, we don't want to interfere with uh, your board meeting," J.T. said. "We'll just take Gabe and go."

"I'm afraid not." Valentine looked at Gabe. "She is like a rose," he murmured. "A rose just about to bloom."

"Can the poetry, Count Chocula," Gabe said.

Valentine winced. "All she lacks is manners," he said.

"Look," I said desperately, "I meant what I said, Valentine. Let her go. I'll do anything."

Valentine drew his head up sharply. "Anything, Zachary?" His nostrils flared. "*Anything?* Because there is the smallest favor you could do for us."

"What's that?" I asked suspiciously.

"The three of you, while perfectly charming, are not enough for us," Valentine said, waving a hand at me, Gabe, and J.T. "We need a more . . . steady supply. Therefore, I would so appreciate it, Zachary, if you would transfer the Undead Express onto a track that functions. That way, we'll be free to pick and choose our victims underground."

"I-I can't do that!" I said. "If you get into the real subway system, you'll be able to see clocks. You can tell when night falls. You'll be able to go aboveground!"

"Of course, that has also occurred to us," Valentine admitted. The crowd of vampires snickered. "Think of it as a bargain you make with us. We would be *so* grateful."

"I can't make that kind of bargain," I said. "I can't turn a trainload of vampires loose on New York! How can you ask me to do that?"

Valentine's hands closed over Gabe's neck. She shivered. "It's simple, Zachary," he said. "It's the only way you can save your friend. Because if you don't, she will be the first one of you to become one of the undead."

14

A Desperate Chance

"Zach, don't do it!" Gabe yelled. "We'll find another way."

"There *is* no other way," Valentine said.

"Zach, you can't!" Gabe said. She tried to struggle her way out of Valentine's grasp, but she couldn't get free. It was strange, because his hands were barely touching her throat.

It was his hands that got me. I could see the bones through the white skin. The veins were flat. No blood ran through them. He was a creature with dead eyes and evil in his heart.

I just couldn't let that happen to Gabe. I couldn't see that dead expression in her eyes. I couldn't see her snarl, and hiss, and laugh in that evil, mocking way.

I met Valentine's gaze. I saw that he knew already what I would say. He'd always been way ahead of me, leading me into the darkness. He had marked me as his victim from the beginning.

"I'll do it," I said.

He let go of Gabe, and she moved away, rubbing her neck.

Valentine smiled. "Excellent choice, if I must say so, Zachary."

"Far out," said Ronnie.

"It's about time," Sims said. "I've been waiting for this for over sixty years. Harv was just a taste of what's to come."

"You know," Pearl said with a sniff, "as long as you mention it, you could have chosen someone with a little more class while you were up there."

"I tried to stop him, Pearl," Valentine said. "But Sims got away from me. It only took a moment, and Harv was one of us."

"He's disgusting," Pearl said. "Those shoes!"

"Now we can climb out of this prison," Sims said. "I can go back to Wall Street—early, before it's light. I can make transactions and then bite my broker. I can be full *and* rich!"

"I can take a night train upstate," Pearl said. "Back to the Falls. I bet there's lots of delicious people there."

I felt sick, listening to them. I turned to

Valentine. "So how do I do it?" I asked.

"Dwayne told us that there's a switching station not too far from here," Valentine said. "It's no longer used. But it still works."

"So why haven't you done this yourself?" I asked.

"Because there is a grate around a corner of the tunnel that leads to it," Valentine said. "As soon as you open the door, it's flooded with light in the day. Those of us who have tried to get there have never returned. As with all those who have tried to escape. That's why we need you. That's why we waited and waited for a living human being to help us. Remember, to us, time is nothing."

"So I'm the lucky one," I said.

"All you have to do is pull a lever to switch the train to another track. I think I would prefer a local line." Valentine tapped his chin thoughtfully. "A line that is not too well traveled. Less attention on us that way."

"But there'll be fewer victims," said Pearl.

"There will be *enough!*" Valentine snarled. He turned back to me. "Now, which line do you think, Zachary? There are so many more, these days."

"It doesn't matter," I muttered.

"Let's try the Number 7 line," Gabe said.

"Number 7?" Valentine asked.

"I've never taken the Number 7," I said.

"Sure you have," Gabe insisted. "We took it to Shea Stadium to see the Mets last summer. Remember? The score was fifteen–zip."

I couldn't believe Gabe was talking about baseball at a time like this. Even if she *was* a fan.

"The Number 7 line," Valentine said. "I like the sound of it."

"Lucky seven," Sims said. The rest of the vampires laughed.

Negotiating the tunnel was a piece of cake. If a vampire had come at night, it would have been easy to get to the switching board.

When I found the switching station, I blew off the cobwebs and eased open the steel door. The switching board was right where Valentine had said it would be. I could even make out the labeling on the switches.

But I hesitated. This was my last chance to save New York. I wasn't even sure if half the people in New York *deserved* saving. Not like Gabe and J.T. did.

That's what got me. Gabe and J.T. were my friends. They were standing right in front of me, living and breathing. I had to save them.

Maybe Gabe had reminded me of that day at Shea Stadium because it had been so great. We'd had so much fun, even though the Mets were in the cellar. Even though we'd eaten too many hot dogs. The whole way home on the train, we were sick . . .

And, just like that, I remembered. The Number 7 train runs aboveground! After passing underneath the East River, it becomes an elevated line. It would burst out into the light. Gabe had been trying to tell me how I could destroy the vampires!

The only thing was, would it work?

I peered overhead at the subway grate. The sun was awfully low. I looked at my watch. It was almost five. The sun was starting to set. Would we get out of the tunnel in time to catch that dying light?

And if the worst happened, if it was dark when we came out of the tunnel, how would I know if Valentine would keep his promise and let us go?

I'm a vampire, Zachary. Evil is my nature.

He had warned me himself that he couldn't be trusted. But I had to take the chance. After all, it was the only chance I had. I pulled the lever to switch the Undead Express to the land of the living.

15

Tunnel of Terror

It took me about ten minutes to get back to Valentine's station. The Undead Express was ready to roll. The vampires were all standing by the windows, looking for me with pale, greedy faces. I even saw Harv at one window. I guessed he'd woken up from his nap.

"Ooooo, I can't wait for dinner!" Pearl said gleefully when I came aboard.

"It's done," I said to Valentine. "Now let Gabe and J.T. go, at least."

"I'm sorry, Zachary, but I can't do that," Valentine said. "Yet. We have to see if you correctly rerouted the train."

"You could have tried the old double cross," Sims said.

"I didn't," I said. I looked at Valentine. "Unlike *some* people, I can be trusted."

But Valentine only chuckled. "I'm sure your friends would agree, Zachary. Why don't you take a seat? We're ready to go."

Gabe, J.T., and I sat as far away from the vampires as we could get, which wasn't easy, given that the train was full of them. The train started with a jerk, and the vampires gave a bloodthirsty cheer.

"Did you do it?" Gabe whispered. "Did you switch the train to the Number 7 track?"

I nodded. "But it's five-fifteen," I whispered back.

"So?" Gabe asked.

"Almost sunset," I said.

"Oh," she said.

"What's going on?" J.T. asked.

But Valentine looked over, so I pressed his leg so he'd be quiet. I could feel his knees knocking together. Gabe's hands were twisted together in her lap.

"Listen, you guys," I said. "I'm really sorry. It's my fault."

"What are you talking about?" Gabe said. "We're the ones who didn't believe you about the Undead Express."

"But why should you have?" I said. "I lied to you about the Knicks games and the safari thing and everything."

"Put a sock in it, Zach," Gabe said. "It doesn't matter anymore. I'm just glad you're back with

112

us." She slipped her hand into mine. It was comforting.

It was nice that Gabe said it didn't matter whose fault it was. But I knew it *did* matter. Maybe I had gotten just a little bit smarter. I knew that *talking* about changing your bad habits wasn't even half the battle. You had to *do* it. I was always talking about something. I talked too much, and some of what I said wasn't even true. So who could I blame when people stopped listening?

Then and there, I promised myself that I'd never stretch the truth—okay, *lie*—to my friends again. Or my parents. Or even Mrs. Nowicki. No matter how many times the Mixmaster called me a wimp.

I knew I wasn't a wimp, but I *had* been a fool. I had trusted the wrong person. I looked over at Valentine. He was standing at the back of the subway car, staring out at the black tunnel. Probably planning whom to feast on first, I thought. Or maybe hoping for some interesting vampires to talk to. Valentine had been right about one thing. I could see how he could get sick of Ronnie and Pearl, not to mention Sims. I was sick of them, and I hardly knew them.

I sneaked a look at my watch. I wasn't sure

when sunset was, but I guessed it was around five-thirty. How much sun did you need to destroy a vampire, exactly? Was just a bit of light good enough? Or did it have to be a full-fledged ray?

Sims rubbed his hands together and smacked his lips. "Can't wait for supper," he said, eyeballing us hungrily. "It will be so nice to have such good friends for dinner." He laughed, and Pearl joined in, giggling. It was like they were all headed for a party. I guess they were. A dinner party. And it looked like we were going to be the appetizer.

"What do you mean?" J.T. asked. "You said you'd let us go if Zach switched the train."

Sims looked at Pearl. "Did we say that?"

Pearl put a finger to her temple. "Did we? I can't remember."

"Wow. I completely spaced it out," Ronnie said. He drooled onto his fringed vest.

"Valentine!" I cried. "You made a bargain!"

Slowly, Valentine turned from the window and looked at me. "It's almost over, Zachary," he said. He turned and looked out at the blackness. "Almost over."

"Well, *that's* reassuring," J.T. said.

"He won't save us," Gabe said. She shot me a frightened glance.

"Are we under the river yet?" Gabe whispered.

I shrugged. I didn't know. All I knew was that somewhere above us the sun was slipping below the horizon. And the sun was our only chance.

The train roared on, faster and faster. The bulbs swung against their cages. Suddenly, Gabe squeezed my hand. And then I saw that the light was changing outside the windows. What had been pitch black was now dark gray. As we watched, hardly breathing, the gray lightened.

"Hey!" Sims said. "What's going on?"

"It's lighter," Pearl said. There was fear in her voice.

I looked over at Valentine. His hands were clasped behind his back. He didn't move, or turn. And he didn't seem surprised. He stared out at the growing light.

"Wait a second!" Sims said. "That dirty double-crossing—"

Suddenly, the train shot out of the tunnel into the open air and the bright orange fire of the setting sun streamed in. It lit up the seats and sent tongues of flame-red light licking at the walls.

Pearl screamed. She held her face in her hands and rocked back and forth. "Nooo!" she wailed. "Stop! Noooooooo!"

Ronnie jumped up, his ponytail flying. He pounded on the compartment door. "Stop the train! Stop!" The door banged open and the conductor fell out on top of him, howling in anguish.

Sims started down the car toward me, his face full of rage. His lips were drawn back over his pointed yellow teeth. I shrank back as he rushed down the car, a black silhouette against the orange sun. His arm reached out to grab me.

"Zach, watch out!" Gabe screamed.

But suddenly, Sims's legs crumpled beneath him. He fell over Pearl, who was writhing on the floor. Dwayne and Harv were face down, moaning.

It was terrible to watch. The train rattled farther and farther into the light and air, as the vampires' flesh bubbled and melted off their bones. Their shrieks became shriller and shriller, until we put our hands over our ears. The bones glowed briefly red in the light, then turned to dust.

I turned to look at Valentine. He was the only one left standing. He had turned to face forward and now stood straight and tall, the setting sun blazing behind him. It looked as though he was standing in a ring of fire. The orange light danced on his cape and lit the ends of his hair.

Then, slowly, he gave a deep shudder and went down on one knee. Then the other. Finally, he fell forward. His hands were out to block his fall, but they crumbled, and his face hit the ground.

He lifted his head and looked toward me. For the first time, I saw something human flicker in his eyes. He opened his mouth, trying to speak. I had to lean over to hear him.

"Thank you," he said.

Then his bones turned into dust, and he was at peace at last.

16

Rest in Peace

I knelt over what had been Valentine. There was just an old suit and a cape with a faded brown satin lining. I picked up the cane that Valentine had called his stick.

Now I knew he had realized all along that I would route the train to an aboveground track. It was the only way he could protect Gabe, J.T., and me from Sims and the rest of the vampires. He *wanted* to destroy all of them. He wanted to free them. And himself.

"Maybe we were friends after all," I said.

"Uh, Zach?" J.T. called nervously. "Could we figure all this stuff out later? Because right now we've got a problem."

I looked up.

"How are we going to stop the train?" Gabe asked.

Dropping the cane, I sprang to my feet. We were on a train rattling away at who knows how many miles per hour. If we sped through a station we could be in big trouble. We could crash into another train, or go too fast on a curve.

We were on an elevated track. Far below, lights were coming on in the buildings along a broad avenue.

"We have to slow it down!" J.T. shouted over the noise of the train.

I hurried forward, kicking through the clothes of the vampires. They were already starting to decay. Pearl's skirt looked like a rag, and the bright ribbons on her hat were faded and torn.

I kicked aside the conductor's uniform and went into the small compartment. I stood uncertainly in front of the controls.

"Try pushing the one on the left back," Gabe suggested.

I pushed the lever, and the train raced forward with a roar.

"Not that way!" Gabe screamed. "Toward you!"

I pulled back on the lever, moving it toward me. The lever clicked into a gear, and the train slowed down slightly.

"Whew," J.T. said. He turned to Gabe, "How'd you know to do that?"

"It was in the research I did about the old

subways," Gabe said, peering through the window. "There's a station ahead. And it looks like there are people waiting."

"What should we do?" J.T. asked. "What if a conductor is there, or the transit police?"

"I'll pull up at the far end of the platform," I said. "Then we'll make a run for the stairs."

The train rattled toward the station. I could see people standing on the platform. They looked at the train. I watched as some of them did a double take and pointed it out to their neighbors. I wished they'd all go back to reading the *New York Post*.

My hands were sweaty, and they slipped on the controls. The train went into a higher gear.

"Zach! Slow down!" J.T. shouted.

"I know," I muttered. I pulled back on the lever and the train reduced speed. I pulled some more. The train slowly moved into the station. I waited until we were almost at the end of the platform, then pulled the lever all the way toward me. The train slowly slid to a halt.

We practically fell over each other trying to get out of the tiny space. When we got to the doors, we saw that I'd overshot the platform by a few feet.

"The back door," I said. "Hurry."

We ran through the train, jumping over the

clothes. I stopped where Valentine had fallen and picked up his stick. Then I followed J.T. and Gabe to the back door. We pushed it open and came out on the little platform.

"Cool train," a guy in a sweatshirt said. "Where did it come from?"

Gabe vaulted over the railing and landed on the platform. J.T. and I followed. "The transit museum," I said.

A transit cop hurried toward us. "Hey, kids!" he yelled.

"Gotta go," I said, and we took off, rushing past him.

We clattered down the stairs and ran across the avenue. We ran until we were out of breath.

"He didn't follow us," Gabe said, looking behind her.

"That was close," J.T. said, holding his side. "Gabe, that was a maximum cool move, to think of the Number 7 line."

"You said it," I said. "You're our hero, Gabe."

"You were really brave, guys," Gabe said. "I thought I was going to lose it before you came."

"I feel great!" J.T. said. "I feel like I could take on the Mixmaster."

"Don't push it," Gabe said with a grin.

I looked at my watch. "Would you consider taking on my dad? He's going to fry my brains and eat them for breakfast. It's five-thirty. What am I going to tell him?"

"We'll think of something on the way home," Gabe said. "If we can get out of a train full of vampires, we can get out of anything."

I grinned at Gabe and J.T. All of a sudden, I realized that something was different. Their faces seemed clearer somehow. It was almost like a fog had been between me and the rest of the world. Maybe Valentine wasn't the only one who'd been freed.

"It's dark already," J.T. said. "We're *all* going to be in trouble soon. We'd better hurry."

Gabe frowned. "We probably shouldn't take the subway back home from that station. That guy saw us."

"We could follow the tracks to the next station," I suggested.

"Good idea," Gabe said, and we started to walk.

In only a few blocks, we came to the next station. Darkness had fallen like a black curtain, and the streetlamps glowed cozily overhead.

Gabe stopped and turned to me and J.T. "I just thought of something. If there was *one* train of vampires, why couldn't there be more? The subway is a perfect place for vampires."

"It *is* always night there," I said.

"And there are a million places to hide," J.T. said.

We exchanged glances.

"Nah," we said together.

I noticed a man standing at the subway entrance. He was dressed in a suit and carrying a briefcase.

"Excuse me, sir. Does this train go to the city?" I asked.

"Yes, it does. It's an express," he said. He smiled at us. His teeth looked a little too long and pointy. And did I smell something rotten?

"I'll show you the right platform," he said. "Follow me."

He went up the stairs. He stopped in the shadows of the landing and looked back down at us. The light of the streetlamp hit his dark eyes, making them glitter.

"Come," he said.

I swallowed. Then I turned to Gabe and J.T.

"Bus pass, anyone?" I said.

Don't miss the next book in the
Shadow Zone series:
GOOD NIGHT, MUMMY!

The mummy climbed out of the coffin.

"Look out!" I yelled. But since it was a video, the actor couldn't hear me. I muted the sound and covered my eyes.

I wrinkled my nose as a faint, mildewy scent wafted past. It was like a towel that's been left in a wet heap for three or four days.

Whump! There was a muffled thud behind me.

All of a sudden I got this prickly feeling on the back of my neck. I could sense a presence.

And it didn't feel like Mom.

I really, *really* didn't want to turn around. But I did.

As soon as I had, I wished I hadn't.

Standing behind the couch, its arms stretched out to within an inch of my face, was a *mummy!*